"Would you mind holding this in place?"

He walked over. She was looking up at him. The glow of her honey-toned face, her eyes the color of rich molasses slow dancing with him and the gloss of her lips all merged into an irresistible portrait of desire. He imagined them together, him braced above her and her staring up at him with that same hungry look of anticipation.

"Would you?"

He blinked, cleared his throat. "Do you always carry around a measuring tape in your purse?" he grumbled. He planted the tip of his shoe on top of the end of the tape, holding it in place.

Lexington slowly rose, and when she did, they were so close he could count her feathery lashes. Her intoxicating scent filled his senses and washed everything else in the room away.

The corners of her eyes crinkled as her smile spread and revealed a row of perfect white teeth. "I was a Girl Scout, Mr. Grant. I'm always prepared."

He could easily wipe that challenging smile off her lips with just one kiss.

* * *

Strictly Confidential by Donna Hill is part of The Grants of DC series.

Dear Reader,

For those who have followed my Grants of DC series, let me introduce you to Montgomery Grant—Washington's mover and shaker in inner-city real estate development and one of the Chocolate City's most eligible bachelors. But every great Grant man needs a woman who can match him stroke for stroke—enter international architect Lexington "Lexi" Randall.

From page one, the sizzle between Montgomery and Lexi doesn't fizzle, even after the last page is read (guaranteed). But in between sultry workdays and steamy nights, the secret of Lexi's return to the States could be the one thing to destroy the relationship of her dreams and her job on Montgomery's project, which could solve all her problems. Secrets. Betrayal. Perfect ingredients for a page-turning romance!

When I brought Montgomery and Lexi together, I wanted to give readers two characters who, while they leaped off the page, were also two people they could identify with, including what they are both fighting for—affordable housing, stable communities and an embrace of Black culture.

Montgomery and Lexi have their hands full, with each other and the changes in the world around them. I'm so happy you are here to share their journey and cheer them on.

Until next time,

Donna

DONNA HILL

STRICTLY CONFIDENTIAL

HARLEQUIN®
DESIRE™

ISBN-13: 978-1-335-73526-3

Strictly Confidential

Recycling programs
for this product may
not exist in your area.

Donna Hill began her career in 1987 writing short stories for the confession magazines. Her first novel was released in 1990, and since that time, she has more than one hundred published titles to her credit and is considered one of the early pioneers of the African American romance genre. Three of her novels have been adapted for television. She has been featured in *Essence*, the *New York Daily News*, *USA TODAY*, *Today's Black Woman* and *Black Enterprise*, among many others. Donna is a graduate of Goddard College with an MFA in creative writing and is currently in pursuit of her doctor of arts in English pedagogy and technology. She is an assistant professor of professional writing at Medgar Evers College and lives in Brooklyn, New York, with her family.

Books by Donna Hill

Harlequin Desire

The Grants of DC

Strictly Confidential

Harlequin Kimani Romance

For the Love of You
Surrender to Me
When I'm with You

The Grants of DC

What the Heart Wants
Forever Mine

This novel is lovingly dedicated
to all the readers who have loved and
supported my work for thirty-one years!

Thank you!

One

Lexington Randall sat behind the wheel of her leased red Mercedes GLC coupe. Parked across the street from Essex House, she monitored the early morning comings and goings. From her vantage point the traffic was mostly workmen. The building was a run-down tenement that had for years been left to rot. Every architect and contractor worth their LLC had responded to the request for proposals and were vying for the opportunity to work on a project that was destined to reshape this forgotten urban enclave of Washington, DC. According to the details in the RFP, the vision was to turn this eyesore into an upscale ten-story living and social complex. Wind of the plan had already stirred a serious buzz in DC.

Lexington slid on her Versace sunglasses, opened the door of the Benz and stepped out into the balmy, overcast April morning. A layer of clouds weakened the warmth of the sun. She pulled the shawl collar of her white wool jacket up around her neck. She leaned against the side of her car and took a slow visual stroll up the hard edges, around the curves and gaping openings on the body of brick and steel. Her pulse kicked up a notch. The possibilities were a serious turn-on. *Hmm, what she could do with this building.* She ran her tongue along her bottom lip.

Since taking over Randall Architect and Design LLC from her father and namesake, she was determined to establish herself as a premiere architect on this side of the ocean, and return the company to one of respect and prominence. Randall Architect and Design LLC was the only Black-owned architectural and design firm in the city, and the only one headed by a woman—*at least for now.* When she'd returned to the States last week from her three-year stint in Europe, she was devastated to discover how bad things were with the business. The company was barely afloat. No one knew yet, but they'd begun the paperwork to file for bankruptcy. Her brother, Maxwell, never wanted to run the company. He'd rather spend his time on the arm or in the bed of one beautiful woman after the other. The result was now the near collapse of the company. Her father had kept that little secret from her until he couldn't any longer. Landing this contract with MG Holdings would provide the financial fuel that Randall Architect and Design LLC needed to survive until she decided what to do. She folded her arms. And she would do whatever was necessary to land this deal. *Whatever.*

"Gonna take a lot to make that into something."

A raw morning voice came from behind her, that kind of voice that woke you up after a long night of hot sex.

Lexington turned. Her breath hitched as an electric tremor zipped between her thighs. *Oh, my.* She swallowed.

The right corner of his full mouth lifted into a tease. He squinted against the overcast sky, tightening the corners of his eyes. He came around the front of the car and stood next to her, rested his hip on the warm hood. He was taller than she first surmised. And he smelled sooo good. *Damn.* His unbuttoned navy suit jacket blew open revealing a snow-white fitted shirt that contrasted against rich brown skin, and made love to a broad chest and rock hard abs.

He lifted his chin toward the building before bringing a cup of coffee to his mouth. "It'll be the beginning of a major turnaround for the community."

"I think so, too." She angled her head toward him and her gaze got all tangled up with his. *That half grin again.*

"You think so, too, huh?"

She swallowed. "Yes. I do." Her brow arched for emphasis. "I can see exactly how to lay it all out, what redesign is needed and what can be gotten rid of." She waved her hand slowly from left to right.

He chuckled. "You can tell all that from here?"

She slid her shades off the bridge of her nose. "I'm very good at what I do."

His tipped his head to the side. "Is that right?"

"Absolutely."

"And what might that be? That you're so good at?"

He crossed his feet at the ankles, took another sip of coffee and made no attempt to hide his penetrating observation of her.

Heat flashed from her neck and raced to her cheeks. She pulled open the collar of her coat. "I'm an architect. I do this kind of thing for a living."

His silky brows arched above brown eyes that held flecks of amber. "An architect?"

Lexington jutted her dimpled chin. She was accustomed to *that* look, the instant of skepticism. Architecture was still primarily a man's world. It took being better, smarter and, when needed, more ruthless than any and every man in the room to get the recognition that she deserved. What she wanted to do was tell him where he could go with that smug, sexy look he kept throwing her way, but her mother's warning voice of tolerance echoed in her head. *Never know who's gonna come and go in your life. Treat 'em all like they matter.*

He pursed his lips. "Have you submitted a proposal?"

"That's why I'm here today. I was hoping to meet Mr. Grant and give it to him in person."

He studied her for a moment. "Well, Ms...."

"Randall. Lexington Randall."

"Well, Ms. Lexington Randall, today is your lucky day—or not." He extended his hand. "I'm Montgomery Grant."

Lexington mindlessly slid her hand into his. So *this* was the elusive face behind MG Holdings, the golden boy of real estate development who'd effortlessly turned trash into treasure, amassing a fortune and a large footprint in the nation's capital, the one who notoriously avoided the limelight. One of DC's most eligible bachelors or so the rumor went. A sizzle of electricity zipped up her arm as his fingers closed around her palm.

She pressed her glossed lips together to keep from gasping. The grainy news clipping pictures did him no justice. She swallowed. "I intend to make it my lucky day, Mr. Grant." She slid her hand from his and opened the driver's side door, reached in for the folder that contained her proposal. She turned back to Montgomery and extended the folder. "I know this is unorthodox, not following the submission process, but I knew that I'd miss the deadline of noon today if I didn't bring it in person."

Montgomery took the file from her fingertips. "Pretty gutsy, Ms. Randall. I don't do business this way."

Lexington dragged in a breath. "Perhaps this one time, you can set your rules aside. Take a look at my proposal. Compare what I can do and can offer to the other proposals you've received. All I'm asking is the opportunity to be considered." She paused a beat. "I'm confident that when you review my proposal, it will outshine all the others."

Montgomery chuckled deep in his throat. "I definitely admire your confidence." He sighed heavily. "Why is your proposal so late? Working with someone that is on the edge of my time frame is immediate cause for concern."

How much could she tell him? She could not come across as desperate. "I returned from Paris last week. I'd been working on a restoration project."

"I see." His jaw tightened. "Do you have some time?"

Her brow rose in question.

"About an hour, maybe more. I'll give you a tour of the building and listen to your pitch. If I like what I hear I'll consider it *along* with the others."

A slow smile curved her mouth. "I can give you as much time as you need to conclude that I'm the one for this job."

Montgomery laughed out loud. "I like you, Ms. Randall. Now, let's see if your vision can match your bravado."

Lexington drew in a relieved breath, pointed her car fob at her Benz, listened for the chirp and fell in step alongside Montgomery Grant. As they crossed the street she had the oddest sensation that walking next to him was the most natural thing in the world, something they always did.

He strode through the front door that was propped open by a wheelbarrow filled to the brim with worn wood planks and what looked like chunks of concrete.

A man who brought to mind a walking tree trunk approached them.

"Morning, Hank." Montgomery greeted a burly six-foot-plus worker, donned in dusty overalls and a hard hat.

"Morning, Mr. Grant." He tucked a clipboard under his thick arm. "Busy day. Permits came through. The crew is going floor by floor getting rid of debris. But some of the floors are in pretty bad shape, so it's gonna be slow going."

Montgomery nodded thoughtfully then clapped Hank on his broad shoulder. "Oh, Ms. Randall—Hank Forbes, my foreman. This is Lexington Randall."

"Ma'am."

Lexington offered a tight-lipped smile of greeting.

"Listen. I need two hard hats. I want to give Ms. Randall a short tour of the property."

"Sure thing." He turned. "Winston!" he shouted. "Winston! Bring me two hard hats," he called out when he'd gotten Winston's attention. "Want me to send someone along with you, Mr. Grant?"

Montgomery tucked in a grin. "Naw. Pretty sure I can handle it. But thanks. Besides I need to put my eyes on what's done and what needs to be done."

Winston, who was a head shorter than Hank but just as solid and wide, appeared with two hard hats. "Morning, Mr. Grant."

"Thanks. Morning. How's everything going?"

"Good. No complaints. Lotta work. But that's a good thing."

"I'll let you get back to it," Montgomery said with a lift of his chin.

Winston gave a brief nod to the trio and strode away.

Montgomery handed Lexington a hard hat. He gave her another long, lazy head to toe once-over. "Can't use the elevator. You good with climbing ten flights in those?" He led with the tip of his nose toward her three-inch heels.

He might have been looking at her red-bottom shoes but she felt his eyes stroking her legs. The stare was so strong it pushed aside the opening of her car coat and lifted the hem of her knee-length skirt. The tiny pearl between her folds jerked to attention. She shifted her weight. "I'll be fine. Thanks." Hopefully the exertion of the ten-story trek and the walk-around would get her refocused on the job and not imagining what Montgomery Grant's lips would taste like.

He put the hat on his head. "We'll start at the top and work our way back down."

Lexington nearly choked at the comment.

"You okay?"

Her cheeks flamed. "Yes. Absolutely. Just a little dust."

He studied her for a moment. "Good point. Let me get us a couple of masks." He walked away and over to the group of workmen, returning moments later with two blue masks. He handed one to Lexington.

"Thanks."

"Ready?"

He didn't wait for her response but started off toward the west stairwell.

She *thought* she was ready when she brazenly posted herself in front of his building. Meeting Montgomery Grant didn't totally throw her off her game but it damn sure got her wobbly. *Get your head back in play, girl, and not on the picture of you and him tangled in some sheets.* "Lead the way."

Montgomery adjusted the hard hat on his head. Yet even with the armor of a suit, tie and construction protection he felt the heat of her pierce right through him. Whatever that scent was that floated around her scrambled his thoughts to a point where he was giving a potential employee a personal tour that clearly bruised the rules of fair play. This was not how he rolled. One thing he prided himself on was being fair and transparent. This little excursion was all kinds of wrong. Unfortunately, at the moment, he didn't give a damn. He wanted to get to know this bold, sexy woman that utterly intrigued him.

They reached the tenth-floor landing. A team of three workers had fashioned an assembly line to pass debris and load it into huge metal bins.

"Watch your step," Montgomery instructed.

She pulled the mask away from her mouth. "I'd take out all the walls on the ground floor," Lexington said instead. "Front to back and across." From her purse she'd taken out a notebook and was furiously making notes. She looked up at the ceiling then walked in a grid-like pattern across the battered wood floors, murmuring under her breath and nodding her head. "Reconfigure the layout so that the entire interior is circular."

"Circular?" He frowned.

She laughed, held up her hand. "Not the rooms themselves. The landings on each level would surround the ground floor in a circular fashion. I'll draw it up and show you what I mean."

He shot her a look, ready to challenge her, but her eyes seemed to sparkle and those lips… "Let's keep going," he grumbled. He led the way down a narrow hall and opened what had once been an apartment door at the end of the corridor.

The stenches of garbage, sewage and mold were living things that hunched in corners, leaned against gouged walls, crept along rotted floorboards and reached out to cling to all who entered.

"We should have put on coveralls," Montgomery said, his voice muffled by the mask. "This building turned into a flophouse after it was abandoned. Took us months to get everyone out and get the place boarded up." He crossed the front of the space to another door and turned the knob. The knob came off in his hand. He snorted a laugh and tossed it aside. The door swung slightly inward, squeaking on rusty hinges. He pushed it fully open.

The stench was overwhelming. The room was littered with old mattresses, filthy sheets, and buckets containing who knows what.

Montgomery took a look over his shoulder at Lexington and she seemed totally unfazed. She was walking around and taking notes as if she was on a tour of the Eiffel Tower in Paris. *Interesting.*

"In the RFP it states that half of the building will be residential and the other hotel-style, with a restaurant, gym and a spa. Correct?"

"Mmm-hmm." He slid his hands into the pockets of his slacks to keep from reaching out to test if the tumble of auburn hair that haloed her face was as soft as it appeared.

"Ambitious," she murmured. "But doable." Her eyes roamed the room. She walked ahead of him to another room similar to the one they'd left then off she went to the bathroom.

All of the fixtures were gone. Nothing was left to indicate what it once was except for the pipes that came out of the walls.

"Mind if I take some measurements?"

He blinked, frowned. "Measurements. Uh…" He shrugged. "Sure, I suppose so."

"Great." She led the way back to the front. She dug in her purse and took out a measuring tape wheel. She walked to the corner of the room, got on her haunches and stuck the end of the tape in the corner. She glanced over her shoulder and lowered her mask. "Would you mind holding this in place?"

He walked over. She was looking up at him. Her honey-toned face glowed, her eyes the color of rich molasses slow danced with him and the gloss of her lips all merged into an irresistible portrait of desire. He imagined them together, him braced above her and her staring up at him with that same hungry look of anticipation.

"Would you?"

He blinked, cleared his throat. "Do you always carry around a measuring tape in your purse?" he grumbled. He planted the tip of his shoe on top of the end of the tape, holding it in place.

Lexington slowly rose and when she did, they were so close he could count her feathery lashes. Her intoxicating scent filled his senses and washed everything else in the room away. His cock jerked to attention. *Damn, he wanted to touch her. Just once.*

The corners of her eyes crinkled as her smile spread and revealed a row of perfect white teeth. "I was a Girl Scout, Mr. Grant. I'm always prepared."

He could easily wipe that challenging smile off her lips with just one kiss, then she'd see who was really in charge.

The more he watched her work, going from floor to floor, room to room, and listened to her ideas, the more intrigued he became. She certainly seemed to know what she was doing and he actually liked the ideas that she'd come up with. They totally fell in line with his vision. They were as in sync as if they'd always worked together. It was unnerving.

More than an hour later they returned to the ground floor. The crew was in full work mode, moving barrels and bins of debris at a steady pace.

Montgomery returned the hats to a stack on a table and tossed their masks in the trash. They stepped outside and both of them simultaneously took a lungful of air, turned to each other and broke out laughing.

"Yeah, it was pretty bad in there," Lexington said over her giggles.

"You took it like a champ, though," he said, reveling in the sound of her laughter.

Her lids fluttered. "Well, thank you. Really. I know that you went out of your way and against protocol, but I truly appreciate it." She stuck out her hand.

Montgomery glanced down at the long, slender fingers and wanted to bring them to his lips. He covered them with his own hand instead. That would have to be enough. For now.

"Not a problem, as long as it stays between us. I wouldn't want to ruin my hard-ass reputation."

"I can't imagine that anyone would think that about you, Mr. Grant," she said, her voice as light as the clouds above.

He rocked his jaw, cleared his throat. "I'll take a look at your proposal," he said, holding up the folder that he'd kept with him like a talisman. "And get back to you. Or someone from my office will."

She nodded. "Thank you. I'll draft up some sketches that I'd be happy to show you."

He paused a beat. "Let's get through the proposal process, see how that goes. You're already at an advantage having taken the tour. It wouldn't be fair to the others to tip the scales any further. I'm sure you understand."

"Of course."

"Thank you for stopping by, Ms. Randall."

"Mr. Grant." She gave a short nod of her head, turned and crossed the street to her car.

Montgomery stood there and watched her every move; the way her legs flexed as she walked on those sexy heels, the way her coat swung around her knees, how her hair blew in the wind, the way she slid behind the wheel giving him one last peek at those legs that he wanted wrapped around his back... He watched until the red-hot car and its even hotter driver were out of sight.

"Hey, boss."

Montgomery turned, smiled at his project manager. "Gabe. Morning."

Gabriel Martin came to stand shoulder to shoulder beside him. "Was that Lexington Randall that I just saw?"

Montgomery angled his head in Gabriel's direction. "Yes. Why?"

"Wow, so that was her. I haven't seen her in—" he frowned "—going on three years or more."

His brows tightened. "Really? How do you know her?"

He adjusted his hard hat. "Uh, dated a while back. Went to MIT together," he said almost wistfully then switched gears. "There's a couple of things I want to

go over with you if you have some time this morning
or late this afternoon."

"Yeah, uh, I actually have a meeting in a half hour.
Why don't you come by the office say around three?"

"Perfect. See you then." He turned and went back
inside.

For several moments Montgomery stood there, processing the past hour topped with Gabriel's revelation.
He strode toward his Lexus parked on the corner, turned
and looked up at Essex House. He couldn't expect that
she didn't have a life before now, but why with someone
that he knew? Just how serious had it been?

Lexington cruised along Pennsylvania Avenue while
trying to take in the sights and reacquaint herself with
the place she'd called home for most of her life. But the
iconic structures and the familiar intersections were
no more than a blur. Her mind kept skipping back to
Montgomery Grant. She shifted in the leather seat. He
was...*hot*. It was the only word that came to mind. It had
been longer than she cared to think about since a man
had, without effort, reached up inside her and found
that sweet spot with just a look, a word, a light touch.
Montgomery did all that and then some.

A car horn blared furiously behind her. She shook
her head, glanced in the rearview mirror then at the
light that was flashing from green to yellow. Damn,
how long had she been sitting there? She held up her
hand in apology to the driver behind her and sped across
the intersection.

What she needed to be concentrating on was securing this project, and not getting busy with Montgomery.

Did he have a significant other? Was it serious? Was he available? *Stop! Just stop.*

She took the next exit and turned onto Stuyvesant Avenue. She pulled to a stop in front of the blue-and-white-framed house that had seen better days. For several moments she stared at her family home from behind the protection of the driver's window.

When she'd come back from Europe her plan was to find a place of her own, but her father insisted that she come home. Besides, he was tired of rambling around in the four-bedroom house alone. Since her mother, Grace, passed away ten years earlier, her father never even dated again, no matter how much she and her brother, Max, insisted. She'd visited as often as she could, but between being away pursuing her graduate degrees and traveling for various architectural projects, her visits home grew fewer and further between. *Did the front steps always sag like that?*

She grabbed her purse from the passenger seat, turned off the car and stepped out. Her dad's fifteen-year-old Jeep Wrangler was parked in the driveway. Dragging in a breath she strutted to the front door and inside.

Lexington slipped out of her coat and hung it on the hook by the front door in the foyer. Her heels popped against the hardwood floors that periodically squeaked beneath her feet.

"Dad!"

"In here."

She followed the sound of his voice to the back of the house. The door to her father's office was partially open.

"Hey," she greeted and stepped inside. "What are you up to?"

Lexington Randall Sr. slowly spun his office chair to face his daughter, a smile beaming across his unlined face. He was pushing seventy-five but didn't look a day beyond fifty. He may not have been able to keep the business financially healthy, but he didn't skimp when it came to his own health and well-being. After losing his wife, Grace, to cancer, he'd spared no expense on natural and organic food, gym memberships, wellness classes—the list went on. Lexi was convinced that her father's obsessions and her brother's lackadaisical attitude contributed to the crumbling of Randall Architect and Design.

She set her purse down on the circular wooden table, walked over and placed a kiss on her father's cheek. She rested her hand on his shoulder and peeked at what he was working on at his drafting table.

"Fooling around with some design ideas for an organic garden out back."

"Hmm."

He glanced up. "Don't like the sound of that." He took off his glasses and set them on the table. He leaned against the stiff back of the leather chair.

Lexington blew out a short breath and took a seat opposite her father.

"Daddy, when you called me and finally told me what was going on, what was on the line, I came back. I came back to help, to make sure that everything you spent your life building, not only your business but your reputation, would not be destroyed. I left a life and a business of my own that was finally taking off."

"And I appreciate that." He patted her hand.

She squeezed her eyes shut for a moment. "Dad. You're a part of this, too. I need to know that you're in this for the long haul. I put my neck out today and took a big gamble. If I can pull it off, I'm going to need you fully on board and engaged in the process. I'm going to have to show some work that has been done over the past two to three years. And I'm going to need to see all the accounts. I need to figure out where things went wrong."

He blinked rapidly, pursed and unpursed his lips beneath his salt-and-pepper mustache. He rested his forearms on his muscular thighs and leaned forward. "You know why I asked you to come back, Lexi? I asked you to come back and fix things as best you could because—" he sighed heavily "—it's not what I want to do. I'm done. Don't have it in me anymore. It's time for me to retire." He lifted his chin. "I thought Max could take over." He shook his head in disgust. "That was a mistake. I didn't want to ask you to come back—especially because of why you left in the first place. But I wanted to leave you and your brother something more than this hundred-year-old house. You can turn this business around, shape it the way you want and be a force to be reckoned with. Make it yours."

Her lips tightened under the flare of her nostrils. She'd been called to save the sinking ship while her father and Max jumped into the life raft. She pushed up from her seat. She blinked rapidly to keep the sting of disappointed tears at bay. What she wanted to shout was, *Is that it? After your golden child Max couldn't handle it, you call in for backup? Always been this way,*

Daddy. Your first thought is never that I can actually do everything I've worked and have trained for. Why? Because I'm a woman? Because I'm not Max! All I've ever wanted to do, all I've ever done was try to please you. To have you see me. Instead she spun away and stormed out.

Lexington slammed her bedroom door. Her entire body vibrated with hurt and outrage. She literally kicked off her heels. One shoe flew across the room hitting the wall and the other landed next to her bed. She pressed her fist to her mouth while she paced. Every man that had ever meant anything to her betrayed her in some way; her male professors that made her feel insignificant but were willing to "go easy" if she maybe stopped by after class, or her brother who always seemed to have a fairy godmother bail him out of the messes he made, including her. Then of course there was Gabriel Martin. She closed her eyes. She honestly thought he loved her, loved her for herself; not for her family name. She'd allowed herself to be open and giving and vulnerable with Gabe, sharing her fears and her secrets. She was going to marry her best friend. Unfortunately, he wasn't only *her* best friend. Gabe seemed to feel the need to share his friendship with Michelle—her ride or die friend since grammar school. Her heart thumped.

Some things never changed. And her own father remained in the number one spot on her list.

She walked over to the window. The sun was beginning to set, casting a soft orange glow across the treetops that hung on desperately to their leaves. She rested her palm against the window frame. She should have known better. She should have stayed in her perfect little apartment in Paris, working on very lucrative restorations projects and building her brand, her bank account and reputation. But no, she'd done what she'd always done; tried to please Daddy.

Now here she was, the de facto captain of a sinking ship. She dragged in a breath. Not on her watch. Hell no. Her brow creased. So, her dad brought her back to save the family name and the company, then dammit that's exactly what she intended to do. But she was going to do it for herself and not a damned other soul. It will be *her* business. *Her* success. And it would start with securing the Essex House project with Montgomery Grant.

Her lids lowered halfway. There was no doubt in her mind that Montgomery Grant had lit a fire in her that had been dormant much too long. She flushed simply thinking of him. But knowing men the way she did she was sure it would be only a matter of time before he betrayed her in some way as well. But in the meantime, she intended to use every one of her God-given gifts, which included skill, brilliance and talent to accomplish what she'd returned to the States to do.

The muffled ringing of her cell phone from the depths of her purse drew her attention. She crossed the room, snatched up her purse and took out the phone. She didn't recognize the number, but maybe it was Montgomery's office.

"This is Lexington Randall."

"After all this time you still kept the same number."

Her knees wobbled. Slowly she eased down to sit on the side of the bed. A furnace of rage lit in her belly and sent intense flames racing through her body.

"What do you want, Gabe?"

Two

Montgomery got behind the wheel of his midnight-blue Lexus and took the ten-minute drive to his office on First Street, SE. From his office window the majestic outline of the US capitol, two blocks away, remained a constant reminder of the power that emanated all around him and fueled his vision.

There was no denying the electric pulse that vibrated in DC. Sure, it was the capital of the country and the seat of authority, but for him it was more than that. DC had a history that the power elite would prefer to keep in the dark. But with the election of the first black president, the opening of the National Museum of African American History and Culture along with the young people that would not remain passive about securing their place in society, the rich history of blacks in America was becoming front and center. He believed deep in his soul that he had a part to play in delivering the message as well. His way was by building an economic infrastructure through real estate; rehabbing decaying neighborhoods and making housing truly affordable for all the people that looked like him. From his construction crew, his vendors, to his office staff—all were people of color. He might not be able to change the inner workings of the political machine, but he could make inroads elsewhere.

Montgomery pulled into the underground parking garage and cruised into his reserved space. He maintained a suite of offices on the seventh floor with a staff of six. Standing in front of the sparkling chrome elevator he mused that less than a decade ago he was working deals out of his home office. Now he was the owner of a boutique hotel, several B and Bs, two apartment buildings and now his biggest project—Essex House.

The elevator doors slid soundlessly open.

"Hey, man, I was just heading out to grab a bite." Sterling Grant, Montgomery's first cousin, best friend and business partner stepped off the elevator. "Thought you were coming in later."

Montgomery let the doors close. "Yeah, that was the plan."

Sterling's smooth dark brows drew close. "You cool, bruh? You look a little out of it."

Montgomery shook the cobwebs away and forced a half grin. "Yeah, I'm cool. Uh, you eating out or coming up to the office?"

"Figured I'd eat out for a change. Why?"

"Think I'll join you. Something I wanna run by you."

"Sure. Jo-Jo's good?" Jo Jo's was the supreme deli

in the downtown DC area. Their sandwiches were legendary, easily giving the iconic Katz's Delicatessen in New York a run for its money.

"Yeah. Getting hungry just thinking about their pastrami," Montgomery said with a grin.

"I hear that."

The two men rode the elevator up to the main level and strode across the marble floor, cutting stunning figures amongst the ebb and flow of lobby traffic. More than a few female heads turned in admiration as the twin towers of *GQ* manliness breezed by them, apparently oblivious to the lusty stares that they elicited. It had been that way with the cousins since their early teens when they began sprouting upward like well-watered trees. The girls at Thurgood Marshall High School had no qualms about pitching themselves onto the paths of Monty and Sterling, offering everything from private homework help to access to bedrooms. The fact that they were both star athletes, Monty with basketball and Sterling with football, only added to their allure. However, with both young men having grown up under the strong hand of the Grant family values, they steered clear of taking advantage of their youthful star power.

Y'all may be some handsome devils. I'll give you that, Montgomery's mother warned them over and over, *but handsome fades and all you got left is the man inside.* The cousins lived by that advice.

"How are things going over at Essex House?" Sterling asked as they waited to be seated.

Montgomery pushed out a breath and shoved his hands into the pockets of his slacks. "It's gonna be a long job. Just getting all of the debris out will take weeks. Can't start anything until that is taken care of. But the crew is on it. I may need to pull in some extra help though."

"Hmm. Well we knew what the deal was when we got into this. It's gonna take a minute. I'll look into what the cost would be to add…maybe ten more guys?"

"Yeah, that would definitely help speed up the process."

"I'll get on it when I go back to the office."

While Montgomery was the visionary and deal maker, Sterling was a numbers man. His MBA in Finance from Howard University was the perfect addition to MG Holdings. Sterling also provided the sobering voice that Montgomery often needed when he wanted to plunge headlong into a promising new property. Buying land and repurposing the property was like a drug to Montgomery. The more property he purchased, the more he needed. He was addicted to the rush of ownership and the leverage that came with it. Sterling on the other hand was addicted to numbers and figuring out how to add more zeroes to the end of those numbers.

They followed the hostess to a table in the rear of the restaurant that was all but packed for the lunch hour rush. The hostess placed a menu in front of each of them and a carafe of water in the center of the table, and promised that their waiter would be with them shortly.

Sterling shrugged out of his steel-gray Ralph Lauren trench coat and draped it across the back of his chair.

They were barely seated when the waiter arrived and took their orders for pastrami on rye with all the fixings and two bottles of Coors.

Sterling reached for the carafe of water and poured a glass. "So, what's going on?"

Montgomery followed suit and took a long swallow. He set the glass down but kept it cupped in his palms. "Earlier this morning at the site, I met this woman."

Sterling's brow rose. "Do tell," he said with a grin.

Montgomery chuckled. "Anyway, she's an architect and she dropped off her proposal for the site."

"Okay? I'm not seeing the problem."

Montgomery dragged in a breath. "She… She's something…" His attention drifted off to the distance.

"Something good or something bad?"

Montgomery's gaze landed on Sterling. "I don't know." He shook his head. "Maaann, I can't explain it."

Sterling leaned back in his seat and appraised his cousin. "Well, I'll be damned. Montgomery Grant, hit by lightning."

"Felt like it. For sure."

"This woman have a name?"

"Lexington Randall. She's the architect for Randall Architect and Design."

"From the look on your face it doesn't seem like it matters much what she does for a living."

"She is really talented. I took her on a tour of the building and her ideas… It was like she read my mind or something."

The waiter arrived with their sandwiches and beer. "Can I get you anything else?" the young man asked.

"Naw, we're good. Thanks," Montgomery said.

Sterling didn't wait a beat. He picked up his overstuffed sandwich and took a healthy bite, then moaned in pleasure.

Montgomery chuckled. "Anyway, I took a quick look at her proposal in the car, and it's the best I've seen."

Sterling wiped his lips with a napkin. "You got a fine woman, smart, sexy and talented who can work on this project. So," he added, "the problem is, you got a thing for her?"

"The problem is she was once involved with my project manager, Gabriel."

Sterling's thick, sleek brows rose a notch. "Hmm," he murmured over the rim of his glass. "How's that square with you, though?"

Montgomery frowned. "Not sure how I feel about it. Awkward for sure and the whole Gabe thing could be a deal breaker. She's definitely talented, but maybe I should save myself the headache."

"Yeah, I hear ya. Probably not worth the trouble." He took a big bite out of his overflowing sandwich, chewed thoughtfully. "Bottom line…" He swallowed and took a long swig of beer. "She's professional, and everyone has a past, including us." He gave a slight shrug. "Up to you."

"Yeah." He heaved a breath. "Anyway, enough about that. Bring me up to speed on the accounts and vendors."

Montgomery needed to put Lexington Randall in his rearview and focus, but dammit, she remained front and center.

When Montgomery returned to his office with all the updates from Sterling still running through his head, he put all of it on the back burner and pulled out the proposal that Lexington had given him that morning.

He flipped the folder open. Countless proposals had

come across his desk, and he could spot a stellar one on first glance. Stellar was the vibe he'd gotten from the first of Lexington's twenty-plus-page proposal. His jaw clenched. What he was looking for was a damned good reason to turn the proposal down—some flaw, some inconsistency, some unrealistic idea, an inflated budget—something. He studied every line, on every page—twice.

He slapped the folder shut. Nothing. He couldn't find a thing wrong with it. The architectural portion of the proposal was airtight and she had the added advantage of offering interior design services, which none of the other companies were able to offer. He would have had to eventually hire a design firm. He pushed out a breath. Now what?

Montgomery spun his chair toward the window and gazed out at the sprawling Chocolate City. Of all the architects in America, it had to be Lexington Randall. Why couldn't she be a dumpy man with a beer gut and nose hairs? Instead—those taunting eyes, lips that looked Georgia peach sweet, long curvy legs and a body that was *Sports Illustrated* front cover–worthy. And the way she smelled made him want to press up against her—inhale her…

His cock jerked. He shifted in his seat. *Lexington Randall.* Go figure. As the old wives' tale goes, "things happen for a reason." Hell if he knew what the reason was this go-round, but who was he to go against "mother wit"?

Lexi eased down on the side of her bed. Her heart banged in her chest and she wasn't sure if it was shock or fury.

"What do you want, Gabriel?"

"Oh, it's back to Gabriel. I remember you only called me Gabriel when you were ticked off at me."

"There is a laundry list of names I could call you, but I don't have the time. Besides, wouldn't my one-time best friend, Michelle, be upset that you're calling me?"

There was a momentary pause.

Gabriel cleared his throat. "That's over. Been over for quite some time."

"Hmm. Too bad."

"I screwed up, LeLe."

"Ya think! And don't you dare call me that." The invoking of his pet name for her hurled her back to a time in her life that she'd spent the last three-plus years trying to forget. She sprang up from the bed and began to pace, with the phone held in a death grip against her ear. "Whatever it was we had to say to each other was said. Lose my number. Goodbye—"

"Please. Wait. Don't hang up."

Her chest heaved. She could feel the sting of rage-fueled tears burn her eyes. She would not cry. Not over this bastard. Never again.

"I know I owe you more than any apology could ever offer. What I did—there's no excuse. It was selfish. I let my ego get the best of me. You didn't deserve that."

She heard his long sigh and squeezed her eyes shut, wishing that she could forever block out the image of him and Michelle together.

"I just hoped that since we might be working together that we should at least find a way to be cordial with each other. I don't want it to be awkward."

Her sleek brows tightened. "What are you talking about now?"

"I saw you today. At Essex House."

Warning lights began to flash but she didn't know exactly where the danger was coming from. "You saw me? So?"

"That's why I called. I saw you talking with Montgomery Grant and he said that you'd submitted a proposal."

The pulse in her temple pounded. *Please no.* "What does that have to do with you?"

"I'm the project manager for Essex House through my company Metro Consultants."

A string of expletives ran the hundred-yard dash through her head and it was through sheer will that they didn't cross the finish line of her lips.

"You know that was always my dream from when we were at MIT together. Opened about two and a half years ago. We've been doing quite well with all of the development going on in DC."

She slowly lowered herself down onto the overstuffed side chair. *This totally cannot be happening.* She'd gone halfway across the globe to forget those gray-green eyes that shifted with his mood, the hair that curled into silky spirals and the chiseled body enveloped in sandy-brown skin. A body that thrilled and thrust into her best friend. She left to forget about the debacle of her relationship with Gabriel, rebuild her sense of worth and create a career for herself, only to return and have that ugly part of her life thrown into her lap.

"Anyway, I wanted to extend the olive branch. If I remember anything about you, you're the baddest woman in the architectural game. I'm pretty sure you'll land the deal."

She rolled her eyes. "Goodbye, Gabriel."

"The offer stays open."

"No thanks."

"Well, good luck with the proposal. I mean that."

"Goodbye, Gabriel." This time she didn't offer the airspace for him to say anything else. She disconnected the call.

She leaned her head back against the chair. She couldn't work with him. She simply could not. That meant—what—letting the family business dissolve? It was either that or she would have to find a deal that was equitable to Essex House. "Dammit!" She slammed her palm against the arm of the chair. She could strangle her brother, Maxwell, for allowing this to happen. Their father, her namesake, had built the business from scratch. Starting off doing rehab for the neighbors, then office spaces, then designing structures from the ground up. It took years to build the solid reputation that Randall Architect and Design enjoyed. She'd been a big part of the growth and success, even as her brother, Maxwell, played the role of being their father's right hand all along the way.

When she'd left the States to go to Paris for a chance of a lifetime opportunity and to shake off the stench that her breakup had left, she was certain that the business was on solid footing.

She walked over to the small desk that served as her mini office and opened her laptop. There was no time like the present to start looking for other opportunities. Maybe if she was lucky she could piece together two or three deals to equal what the Essex House project would have brought in. The hard truth was that if there was not a large influx of capital quickly the business would fold. *Wait until she got her hands around her brother's neck. He could avoid her for only so long...*

Montgomery unfastened the top button of his shirt and loosened his tie. He studied the twenty-seven-inch screen of his Mac desktop that showed the three-dimensional plans and virtual tour for a row of three townhouses, another project that he had in the works. If all went well, the new tenants, who'd been selected from a lottery, would be able to move in within the next three weeks. The homes had one more electrical inspection to undergo in the morning, and he didn't anticipate any issues. The light knock on his office door drew Montgomery's attention away from the stack of documents on his desk. He glanced up. Smiled.

"Yes, Cherise."

"Gabriel Martin is here. He said you told him to drop by."

Montgomery cleared his throat. "Sure. Send him in." He pushed the documents on his desk aside and turned off his computer.

Gabe stuck his head in the open door. "Hey boss."

"Gabe, come on in. Grab a seat." He waved him in.

Gabe walked fully into the office, glanced briefly around before unzipping his jacket and sitting in the chair opposite Montgomery's desk. He crossed his right sneakered foot over his left knee.

"So, bring me up to speed. You wanted to talk." Montgomery leaned back in his seat, as much to give himself some leg room as to assess Gabriel Martin from a new perspective.

"Yeah." He leaned forward and rested his forearm on his denim-clad thighs. "I've been going over the timeline for demo and debris disposal and if we are going to stick to the timeline and not go over budget before we really get started we're going to need more men and additional equipment."

Montgomery nodded. "I've already spoken to Sterling about adjusting the budget for ten new hires. He's been running the numbers. I don't foresee a problem. As soon as he gives me a final figure you can deal with the hiring. But I do want to encourage you to include at least three to four ex-offenders. It's part of our commitment to the reentry program."

Gabriel dragged in a breath and slowly exhaled, pursed his lips.

Montgomery's brow rose. "Problem?"

Gabriel shifted in the seat. "No. I mean this is your project. You want ex-cons on the job…"

"And you have an issue with that?"

"How can they be trusted not to reoffend on the job and cause problems for the entire project and all the workers?"

Montgomery snorted a derisive laugh. "So, basically your position is if you're wrong, you're always wrong and will do wrong again. There's no redemption or second chances in your world."

Gabriel glanced away then back at Montgomery. "Hey." He held up his palms in submission. "I'll do whatever you need to get the job done."

Montgomery rocked his jaw. "Good. When you line up the intended hires, I'd like to see their paperwork."

His brows flicked upward for an instant. "Sure," he conceded. He pushed to his feet. "I'll get right on it." He zipped his jacket. "Any decision on the architectural firm?"

"I should have a decision by the end of the week."

"Randall Architect and Design in the running?"

"Along with all the others," he said noncommittally. "Won't be a problem for you working with them if they are selected?"

Gabriel slung his hands into his pockets. "No. Don't see why." He gave a slight shrug.

Montgomery slowly nodded his head while Gabriel spoke. He inhaled deeply. "So as soon as I get you the budget, I'll be looking for those names. Keep me posted."

"Will do." He turned and walked out.

Montgomery leaned back in his seat, spun it around so that he faced the window. When he'd been in the market for a project manager for Essex House, he'd done his due diligence and meticulously interviewed and researched each company along with his cousin Sterling. They'd both agreed that Gabriel Martin's Metro Consulting was the best choice and the biggest bang for the buck. Although his project résumé was not as long or detailed as some of the others under consideration, the references from Metro's clients outshone all the others. He was rarely wrong about someone, but Gabriel's comments rubbed him the wrong way. However, for the good of the project he would put his misgivings aside for the moment, and hopefully Gabe wouldn't make him regret it.

His immediate dilemma, however, was making a decision on an architectural firm. He needed to make sure that the right head was making the right decision. His body was saying one thing and his good sense another. And good sense dictated that Lexington Randall presented more problems than he was willing to solve. This project was too big and too important to the community and the commonwealth of DC for him to make a decision for all the wrong reasons.

Three

When Lexington emerged from her room, still fuming and slightly shaken from her call with Gabriel, she found the family home down-comforter quiet as if it had snuggled in for a long nap. She peeked out the living room window that faced the short driveway and noticed that her father's Jeep was gone. She pulled in a sigh and let the curtain fall back in place. Just as well, she was still too upset to deal with her father and she didn't want to say anything that she would regret.

She wandered into the kitchen and her stomach, seeming to sense its surroundings, growled in response. "Feed me," she murmured in a gravelly mimic of the *Little Shop of Horrors* plant. "Late lunch it is." She pulled open the fridge and peered inside, pulled out the carton of extra-large eggs, tomatoes, a green pepper, an onion and feta cheese.

Determined to shift her crappy mood, she began to hum some tuneless melody as she cracked eggs, sprinkled in salt and pepper and began to dice the onion, green pepper and tomato before adding them to the whipped eggs. She dropped a dollop of butter into the cast iron frying pan and watched it slowly melt, spreading languidly across the black bottom until the surface gleamed. Her mother always insisted that the only way to fry up a perfect chicken was in a cast iron pan. Her father must have tried to get her mother to use the copper pot set he'd purchased, and then the stainless steel, and her mother would smile with gratitude, kiss his cheek and fawn over the sparkling cookery. Lexington shook her head in amusement. Her mother, Grace, was something else. When she dazzled her husband with that smile and soft southern drawl, he was pure putty, and she went right ahead and did whatever was on her mind to do. The presence of the frying pan after all these years was a testament to her kid-glove tenacity—the embodiment of a steel magnolia.

What advice would her mother have given her about Gabriel? What would she tell her to do now—torn between salvaging the family legacy or her own sense of self-preservation? Grace Randall may have come across as soft and sweet but beneath that gentile exterior was a woman that saw the world and the people in it for who and what they were. She had no problem cutting toxicity out of her life, whether it be friend or family, and would cut you off in such a way that you'd never realize that you'd been sliced. Lexington believed that her mother would have approved of her move to Paris for all the reasons that she'd left. However, Grace Randall's signature raised right brow would be all over her return and the reasons why. She could almost hear her mother's harrumphs barely hidden under her breath.

Lexington used the spatula and slid the omelet out of the skillet and onto a plate and sat down. Maybe it wasn't her responsibility to save the family business. She forked a piece of omelet into her mouth and slowly chewed. The odds were actually against her: Gabriel being the project manager for one, and two, the undeniable attraction she had for Montgomery Grant. Not to mention that although she knew her proposal was stellar, it was borderline late and probably overly ambitious. She stared off into the distance. None of that mattered. She wanted it. She wanted it bad and not for any of the obvious reasons: the family legacy *and* her attraction to Montgomery Grant. She wanted it for *herself.* She wanted to put her stamp on this major project that could reshape the city she'd called home.

A slow smile slid across her lips. The hell with Gabriel Martin. She wanted this job and if she happened to land Montgomery Grant in the process—then so be it.

The sound of the front door being opened drew her attention away from her budding plan. The familiar timbre of her brother Maxwell's voice drifted into the kitchen. She gritted her teeth when his six-foot-two chiseled body filled the frame of the kitchen doorway. That winning smile that he shared with their mother bloomed across his face and lit up the room like midday sunshine.

"Gotta go," he said to whoever was on the other end of his cell phone call. His dark eyes sparkled. "Sis!" He crossed the space in long-legged strides, wrapped her in a bear hug and plopped a kiss on her cheek. He held her shoulders at arm's length. "Looking good. How are you? Dad said you were coming back." He plopped down in the cushioned kitchen chair next to her.

It took all she had not to roll her eyes at her brother, but it was hard as hell to stay angry at Maxwell. That Randall charm radiated from him as easy as the air he breathed. He had the gift of disarming even the staunchest of his critics, including her.

She pushed out a breath of concession, even as she bit back a smile. "Hey, Max."

He rested his arm on the table. "Aw come on, you could sound happy to see me. It's been what—three going on four years since you've been home." His eyes roved the kitchen. "Any coffee?"

"In the pot," she said off-handedly.

He hopped up, crossed over to the counter and filled a cup with coffee then returned to the table.

"So, tell me, bring me up to speed about life in Paris. We haven't talked in a minute."

"I think that can wait."

He frowned and took a sip of coffee.

"What we need to talk about is the state of the family business."

The light in his eyes slightly dimmed. His lashes lowered. "Yeah. About that." He slowly nodded his head. "Business has been slow."

She leaned back and folded her arms. "Oh, really?" She felt her right brow do that thing her mother had mastered. She watched Maxwell's Adam's apple bob in his neck.

"Look, you've been away. Maybe things are cool in Paris, but business is tight on this side of the ocean. Deals fall through. Potential clients don't materialize." He pursed his lips. "It's tough." He looked authentically stricken.

"When I left, the business was totally solvent. We were solidly in the black," she emphasized with a slap of her palm against the table.

"That's all past tense, Lex." He looked into her eyes the way one would to someone who was incapable of understanding what was being said. He reached over and covered her hand. "A lot has changed since you went away." He pushed to his feet and took his coffee cup to the sink. "Maybe it's time to call it a day. Know what I mean?" He turned from the sink to face her. "Salvage what we can."

The whirl of fury began to stir in the pit of her stomach. She got on her feet and to within inches of her brother's face. "You know what, Max, you're right. I intend to salvage this company. I intend to rebuild it and I intend to do it without you. You never wanted this," she said, her tone dismissive. "Fine. But I'll be damned if I'm going to stand by and let your lackadaisical attitude destroy everything that Daddy built." She vigorously shook her head, then poked her brother in the chest. "I'll have my attorney draw up the papers, removing your name from the business."

His eyes widened. He opened his mouth to protest but Lexington put a cork in it.

"Don't even," she said in warning. "You want out. You got it." She whirled away. Her heart banged in her chest, as she prepared for the onslaught of Max's response. She sat back down.

Several moments of silence filled the space between them.

Maxwell came to sit back down beside her. He exhaled a slow breath. "You're right, ya know." He lowered his head. "I never wanted this, at least not the responsibility of it." His shoulders rose and fell in resignation. "This isn't me. The last thing I want to do is run this business."

Lexington felt her stance softening but remained wary as this whole contrite thing he was doing was typical Maxwell. "So…you're good with me taking your name off the company."

"Yeah. Go for it. I haven't contributed anything to the business in forever, *if* ever," he added with a sardonic laugh. He looked at his sister and smiled. "This has always been you and Dad's baby."

She tugged on her bottom lip with her teeth.

"I know you're second-guessing," he said, pointing a finger at her. "You're doing that thing with your lip."

They both chuckled.

"What I'm saying is true and I ain't gonna feel bad if you admit it," Maxwell said.

Lexington sighed heavily. "So what *do* you want to do, Max?"

"Make music."

She frowned. "What?"

"Yeah. I want to produce music and launch new artists. It's what I've always wanted to do, but what I wanted was overshadowed by the business. I've built a studio in my basement and have been recording for about a year. I bill musicians and singers for studio time. I'm working with Meridian Records to bring new artists on board."

She stared at her brother in awe. "Max… I had no idea."

He actually looked sheepish. "Yeah, so that's my thing, big sis. It's what I want. What I'm damned good at."

Lexington slowly nodded her head. "So…tell me all about it. Everything." She propped her elbow on the table and rested her chin on her palm.

Spending the night dreaming about a woman was not an issue that had ever plagued Montgomery Grant. Until now. All night he'd dreamed of Lexington Randall—her smile, the challenge in her eyes, the way her lips puckered ever so slightly before she spoke, and the scent that was barely there and begged one to draw closer to discover the source. He blew out a breath of frustration. He didn't even want to reimagine the perfect body that had entwined with his and the wonders that he'd discovered in his dreams. He was hard just thinking about her.

With a groan, he sat up in bed and rotated his shoulders. He squinted against the sun that beamed in through the bay window of his Georgetown colonial. The windows were the first thing that attracted him to the three-bedroom home. Growing up he'd always been drawn to the bay windows of the library where he'd sit for hours pouring over books on the history of DC, and its construction—much of it by slaves.

He tossed the sheet aside and stood, stretched long and hard until he could feel the ropes of his back muscles expand and contract and his arousal begin to ease. A cool shower would do the rest.

Showered, shaved and dressed, Montgomery filled his traveling coffee mug, grabbed his keys and laptop bag and headed out. Today he needed to make a final decision on the proposal for the architect. He had to put his biases and his attraction aside and make a decision based on what was best for the project. That was the bottom line.

When he arrived at his office he met Sterling coming down the short corridor.

"Hey, man," Montgomery greeted.

They did the whole handshake bring-it-into-the-chest move.

"I've been looking over the numbers, specifically for the additional staffing."

"And?"

They walked stride for stride toward Montgomery's office.

"Good morning gentlemen," Montgomery's assistant, Cherise, greeted. Her gaze lingered a bit longer on Sterling.

"Perfect start to my day." Sterling smiled.

Montgomery noticed the lift in her breath whenever she looked at his cousin. He cleared his throat. "Any messages?"

"They're on your desk. And don't forget your eleven o'clock with Ms. Fields from Frederick Douglass Bank."

Frederick Douglass Bank was one of the few fully

black-owned banks in the DC area that was equipped to handle the kind of account that Montgomery wanted for his business. Although he could easily get more financing from the big commercial banks, part of his business model was building black wealth through housing, employment and partnerships.

He nodded. "Right. Right. Thanks. Why don't we put in an order now for lunch," he shot a look at Sterling, "For four? I'm sure she'll bring someone and I want you in there as well."

"Not a problem. I'll work for food," he joked and flashed a smile in Cherise's direction.

"I'll take care of it."

"Thanks, Cherise." He walked to his office and opened the door. "Make yourself at home as usual," Montgomery teased his cousin.

"Don't mind if I do." He lowered himself onto the two-seated couch and crossed his right foot over his left knee and placed his laptop on the space next to him.

Montgomery sat down behind his desk. "You are not gonna ask her out, are you?"

Sterling frowned. "Who?"

"Cherise?"

He chuckled. "Cherise? You're kidding, right?"

"No. I'm actually not."

"Naw." He frowned and looked genuinely perplexed. He shook his head. "Why would you say that?"

"Then you need to stop flirting with her."

"Flirting?"

"Yeah. Flirting."

"Aww come on man. Me?"

"Yeah you. It's what you do. And it's so second nature you don't even notice. But she does. Trust me."

Sterling's expression shifted from true surprise to contemplation. "I don't want to lead her on. Not my intent. Just being nice."

"Don't try so hard. She's only been here a couple of months. She hasn't grown immune to the Sterling Grant charm yet. She's an excellent assistant and I want to keep it that way. Besides that whole mixing office business with pleasure thing…"

Sterling pushed out a breath. "Duly noted." He slapped his palms on his thighs. "Now, let's talk business." Sterling flipped open his laptop. "I've shifted some numbers around…"

They talked for about an hour finalizing the accounting details on payments due along with their revenue streams. Essex House was going to dig deep into their funds and the need for the additional line of credit from the bank as a security blanket was important if they were to stay on track and remain high above water. One thing that the cousins always agreed on was that they would make whatever sacrifices and contingencies needed in order to stay in the black. They'd seen too many small businesses fold because they took on more financial risk than they could handle, that and bad financial advice.

Montgomery leaned back in his seat, linked his fingers behind his head and grinned. "We're in a really good place."

"Yep." He snapped the laptop closed.

"Thanks to you."

The corner of Sterling's mouth quirked into a half grin.

"Seriously. You know your stuff and you never let me run off the rails with my take over the world view."

Sterling chuckled. "That's true, my brother. Leave it up to you we'd be washing dishes in the big house."

They laughed.

"But it's what we do, man," Sterling said. "You have the vision and that drive and I crunch those numbers to make it happen."

"The perfect team."

"Fo' sho'."

"So, uh…" Montgomery leaned forward. "I need to make a decision about the architect. We have to move on that ASAP."

"Yeah. So…what have you decided?"

He ran his hand across his head. "I know that this is my wheelhouse, but this time I need your input. I don't know if I can be objective."

"Ohhh, you mean about Lexington Randall?"

"Yeah."

Sterling gave a slight shrug. "Hey, I'll take a look. Run her numbers along with all the others and get back to you after our lunch meeting."

"Thanks, man." He opened the drawer under his desk, flipped through the folders and pulled out the one marked "Randall." He came around his desk and handed it to Sterling.

"Not a problem." He pushed to his feet. "For me," he added with a warning tip of his head toward his cousin. "See you at one." He left the office, closing the door softly behind him.

A sudden flash of Lexington's long legs strutting in the those red-bottom heels jerked him to attention.

The intensity of the image hitched his breath. *Damn.* He shook his head to dispel the image and temper the throb in his pants. He had to get this out of his system one way or the other.

Montgomery's intercom buzzed.

"Yes, Cherise?"

"Ms. Fields is here. I set her up in the conference room."

"Thanks. Let Sterling know. I'll be there in a minute. Oh, did she come alone?"

"Yes, she did."

"Hmm, okay. Thanks." He got up from his desk, grabbed his jacket from the back of his chair and walked out to the conference room at the end of the hall.

When Montgomery pulled the door open he found Sterling and Loretta Fields already in conversation. The buffet behind the ten-foot conference table was lined with sandwiches, salad and a charcuterie platter, a pitcher of iced tea and one of water.

"Ms. Fields," Montgomery greeted, crossing the room with his hand extended. Loretta Fields was nothing like he imagined. She looked more like a cover girl than a finance manager. Her sleek shoulder-length bob framed a coco-brown face and large dark brown eyes. She was tall, slender and the navy pantsuit was sexy in a way that wouldn't be associated with banking.

Loretta Fields set down the glass of iced tea in concert with the slow smile that emphasized lush red lips. "Mr. Grant. Good to finally meet you in person."

Montgomery closed his hand around hers. "You,

too." He started to pull his hand away and met an instant of resistance. "Let's eat and talk."

"Absolutely."

They fixed their plates.

"I heard they've made some management changes over at the bank," Montgomery said.

"We have a new CFO and some of the departments were reorganized, but our mission hasn't changed. We're committed to investing in black-owned businesses."

Sterling held her chair while she sat.

"Thank you," she mouthed, glancing up at him before turning her attention to Montgomery. "How are things progressing with the development?"

"At the moment we're on track." Montgomery settled in his seat with his plate in front of him. He turned his entire essence in Loretta's direction and hypnotically laid out his vision for Essex House, what he knew it would bring to the community; the job opportunities before, during and after construction; and top-of-the-line living, dining and entertainment spaces. "Although as we indicated in our application," he said, smoothly shifting back from salesman to business mogul, "we want more of a cushion to avoid any unforeseen expenses in the coming months. As a businessman the last thing I want to do is to tell my team we have to call off work because we've run out of capital."

"Of course." She reached for her glass and took a sip of iced tea.

"And I'm sure you've seen that we're totally solvent and have never gone into the red on any of our acquisitions or developments," Sterling interjected.

"And we intend to stay that way," Montgomery said. "This project is a much bigger undertaking than our previous work. I'd rather be safe than sorry."

Loretta licked her bottom lip, drew in a breath and slowly exhaled. She linked her slender fingers together on top of the table and looked from one man to the other. "We've thoroughly reviewed your financials and run the numbers for the projected income for Essex House." She paused. "And we believe in MG Holdings and want to see it succeed. Fredrick Douglass Bank is happy to be your financial partner." She beamed a smile.

Montgomery's mouth spread into a grin as he slowly bobbed his head. He stretched his hand across the table. "You've made the right choice."

She settled into his gaze. "I'm sure that I have."

Sterling cleared his throat, interrupting the discernable charge in the air.

Montgomery released her hand, reached for his glass and raised it. Sterling and Loretta did likewise. "To a successful partnership."

"I'll have all the loan documents prepared and sent over for your review," Loretta was saying as she walked alongside Montgomery en route to the elevator.

They stopped in front of the doors. Montgomery pushed the down button. "I'll look out for them."

"The process to get the funds into your account shouldn't take more than five to seven business days once that paperwork is signed."

"That's fine."

"Maybe… I could…bring them to you and we could review them," she gave a slight shrug, "over dinner."

He dipped his head a bit, pursed his lips. "Electronic is fine. I'll go over them with Sterling and if there's a problem or an issue, I'll be sure to reach out."

The elevator doors slid open.

She lifted her chin, blinked. "Of course," she said on a breath. "Have a good day, Mr. Grant." She stepped onto the elevator, turned to face him. "We'll talk soon." The doors closed.

Montgomery shook his head. "Damn," he muttered and walked back toward his office to find Sterling waiting for him. Montgomery closed the door.

"What's with the 'stranger than fiction look'?" Sterling asked.

Montgomery pushed out a breath and gave a short shake of his head. "Ms. Fields offered to bring the papers to me and we could 'discuss over dinner.'" He crossed the room and sat down behind his desk, leaned way back in his chair.

Sterling's brows lifted. "Oh, damn. Seriously?"

"Very." He linked his fingers behind his head.

"You don't think she'll mess this loan up or slow walk it?"

"Crossed my mind. But I want to lean on the side that she's a professional first."

Sterling plopped down in the club chair opposite Montgomery's desk. He rested his forearms on his thighs. "Look, there is no doubt that we could use the financing. But—" he paused, pursed his lips "—we're still in a solid place. I can take a new look at the projections and see where we can scale back if necessary. So, if you're not feeling this whole 'let's talk about it during dinner' thing, don't stress it. We're still good."

Montgomery heaved a slow breath then nodded in agreement. "The last thing we need is self-inflicted complications."

"Speaking of which, I went over the proposal for Lexington Randall."

Montgomery's pulse kicked up a notch at the sound of her name. "And?"

"I have to say... I am impressed. Based on her proposal and projections she would not only come in on time, but just under budget—which of course leaves us wiggle room for any unforeseen problems."

"Okay. I hear a 'but.'" He leaned forward and linked his fingers on top of his desk.

"Well, I didn't have time to do a deep dive into the company's financials, but my cursory review shows that the company, while maintaining a stellar reputation, may have some financial issues."

Montgomery stroked his cheek. "Meaning?"

"It appears that there haven't been any new projects or influx of capital for about a year. Money is going out, but not coming in."

Montgomery frowned. "Expenses?"

Sterling shrugged slightly. "Could be. Hard to tell. According to the public records, it's a family business, mainly run by Lexington Sr. and his son, Maxwell. The daughter is a partner as well but has been out of the picture for a while now."

Montgomery tossed the information around in his head. "Hmm. Maybe that's why she came back—to get them solvent again," he mused almost to himself.

Sterling pushed to his feet. "Whatever the reason, the proposal is solid, the company rep is solid. Now you just need to decide if that's enough for you to keep your head in the game or go elsewhere because you…can't separate 'business from pleasure.'" He gave Montgomery a wink and strode toward the door. "Later."

"Yeah, later," he murmured. He spun his chair toward the window. He could keep it together, keep it professional. She was the best one for the job, she shared and exceeded his vision—in more ways than one.

He leaned over and pressed the intercom.

"Yes, Mr. Grant?"

"Cherise, would you get Ms. Randall from Randall Architect and Design on the phone and find out if she's available to come into the office today. Whatever time is convenient for her."

"Will do."

"Thanks."

Lexington's pulse beat in her veins while she slowly placed her cell phone on the nightstand. She dragged in a triumphant breath and lowered herself to the side of the bed. Montgomery Grant wanted to meet with her. There was no way that he'd invite her to a meeting only to tell her that he'd chosen another company. *You got this, girl.* She pushed up from the bed, planted her hands on her hips before marching over to the closet. What she needed was a banging outfit, just the right touch to seal the deal.

Montgomery checked his watch for the third time in less than twenty minutes. Cherise informed him that she'd confirmed the appointment with Lexington Randall for five thirty. It was five twenty. He slipped on his jacket, ducked into his private restroom to check his five o'clock shadow and do a quick gargle, just as his desk phone intercom beeped. He quickly wiped his mouth and hurried to the phone. He waited a beat then pressed the intercom.

"Yes, Cherise?"

"Ms. Randall is here for your five thirty."

"Thanks. You can send her in."

He licked his bottom lip and buttoned his jacket just as his office door opened.

Lexington stood for a moment framed in the doorway and Montgomery would have sworn in front of all of his boys and on a stack of Bibles that there was this white light surrounding her, blocking out the rest of the world. He blinked away the illusion.

"Ms. Randall, please come in. Thanks for making time on such short notice."

He watched her dark eyes sweep across the expanse of the room and when her gaze settled on him the muscles in his stomach flexed. She crossed the room in what to him felt like slow motion.

He cleared his throat and came from behind his desk. He extended his hand toward one of two matching club chairs. "Make yourself comfortable. Can Cherise get you anything before she leaves for the night?"

"No. Thanks. I'm fine." She unbuttoned her coat.

Montgomery hurried to her side and stepped behind her. "Let me help you with that." He slowly slid the off-white coat off her shoulders and down her arms, inhaling that scent of hers that made him crazy. His eyes closed for an instant. *What was she wearing?*

"Thank you," she said, snapping him out of his momentary trance.

He strode over to the coatrack and hung up her coat, came back and sat in the club chair opposite her.

Lexington crossed her legs. Her fitted black skirt inched up. Montgomery focused his gaze on the tiny pulse beat at the base of her throat, which did him no good whatsoever. The silky white blouse with the deep neckline gleamed against the warm chocolate of her skin. She wore her thick shoulder-length hair up in a knot on top of her head. The wiry tendrils sprang around her face in organized chaos making him imagine what she would look like fully tousled after a night of hot sex.

"So, I'll get right to it." He draped his arm along the back of the chair. "We received some outstanding proposals for this project, and it was difficult to come to a decision."

Lexington shifted in her seat.

Montgomery cleared his throat. "However, after careful consideration we feel that Randall Architect and Design is the company that shares our vision—and comes under budget," he added with a half grin.

Lexington's sigh was audible. A smile lit fire in her eyes. "Thank you. I know the competition was steep and I appreciate that you gave me the opportunity to even be in the running. You won't be disappointed."

"I'm sure that I won't." He watched the rise and fall of her chest. He slapped his palms against his thighs. "So… I'll have the final contract drawn up for your review this week."

She nodded. "Great."

An awkward moment of silence hung between them. Lexington shifted in her seat.

"Actually, if you have some time we could go over the draft."

"Now?"

"I mean we could, but if you have other plans—"

"No. I'm free."

"Great." He went to his desk phone and pressed the intercom. "Cherise. Would you print out a copy of the draft of the design contract for Essex House?"

"Right away."

"Thanks. Oh, as a matter of fact print two copies please." He disconnected the call. "Um. Would you mind talking over an early dinner?"

She slowly uncrossed her legs. "No. Not at all."

Montgomery ripped his gaze away from the silk of her legs, but not before he saw them raised and wrapped around his bare back. He adjusted his tie. "Ever been to Bottomline?" He turned off his computer.

She dipped her head to the side. "Don't think that I have." She stood.

"Good. I think you'll like it."

"I'll have to take your word for it," she said, allowing a slow smile to move across her mouth.

"We can grab the contracts on the way out." He came around and helped her with her coat. "I've always been a man of my word," he said, almost in her ear.

Her head swiveled behind her and their gazes collided. The air hitched between them.

The light tap on the door severed the moment.

"Mr. Grant, here are your—" she stopped short, looked briefly from one to the other "—copies."

"Thanks, Cherise."

"No problem." She handed over the folder. "Good night." She offered a tight smile and slipped out.

Lexington draped the straps of her mango-colored Kate Spade purse over her left wrist.

Montgomery walked to the coatrack and lifted his jacket from the hook. He opened the office door and walked out after her.

Four

Montgomery held open the building's exit door and they stepped out into the falling dusk of the spring evening. The last streaks of sunlight filtered through the clouds turning them into puffs of dusty rose and soft orange above the rooftops.

"It's on the next block," Montgomery said as he slipped into his jacket. He lightly pressed his hand to the small of her back to guide their direction and took up his spot with Lexington walking on the inside.

"You can always tell a real gentleman by how he walks with a woman down the street," she said, giving him a quick sidelong glance.

He smiled. "One of the many rules my father ensured my brothers and I lived by."

"Brothers. Plural. How many?"

"Two."

"Where do you fit in?"

"Youngest."

They stopped in front of the Bottomline Lounge. He pulled open the door.

"Spoiled?" she teased and stepped inside.

"According to my brothers," he said with a hint of laughter in his voice.

They stepped up to the hostess's lectern.

"Good evening, Mr. Grant. Welcome to Bottomline. Two?"

"Yes. Please, Heather. Uh, do you have anything in the private dining space open?"

The young woman pursed a grin. "Let me see what I can do." She strutted away, her blond ponytail bouncing in step.

"Should I be impressed?" Lexington asked with a quizzical lift of her brow.

He slid his hands into the pockets of his slacks. "Naw. Not really. I just come here a lot. Usually with my business partner—my cousin Sterling."

"I didn't realize that MG Holdings was a family business."

"Sterling is like the fourth brother. We grew up together. Only six months apart. Went to the same college. We've been shoulder to shoulder since we were kids. When I started out in real estate, he went down the rabbit hole of numbers." He chuckled. "Made sense for us to join forces since numbers give me hives."

"Nothing like my brother," she said drolly.

"Oh?"

"I'd rather not get into it."

He gave a slight shrug. "No problem."

Heather returned. "I have that table for you, Mr. Grant."

"Perfect. Thank you."

"Follow me."

She led them through the softly lit interior to the back of the restaurant that was sectioned off by beveled glass. She placed two menus on the table. "Your server will be with you shortly. Can I get you anything from the bar while you wait?"

Montgomery held the chair for Lexington. "I'll take a bourbon on the rocks. Ms. Randall?"

"Hmm, white wine, please." Martinis were her go-to drink but she didn't dare lose her head around Montgomery Grant. She didn't trust herself.

"Right away." Heather walked off.

Lexington sat. She glanced around. "Very nice. I'm almost impressed." She grinned.

Montgomery ran his tongue along his bottom lip and she wondered what he would taste like with a hint of bourbon on his mouth. Coming here might be under the guise of business but she knew he was feeling her just as much as she was feeling him. Each time his eyes landed on her, heat whipped through her veins. And it was no accident that he made a point of nearly whispering in her ear each chance he got. She shifted in her seat. But this was all about business. She needed to keep her head on straight no matter how hard being so close to him made it for her.

Montgomery placed the folder with the contracts on the table and picked up the menu. "The jumbo scallops and fettuccini are excellent," he offered while he scanned the menu.

"Hmm, sounds good. And a house salad."

The waiter arrived, placed the drinks on the table and took their orders.

Montgomery lifted his glass. "To new business."

Lexington touched her glass to his. "New business."

Montgomery took a swallow of his bourbon then he opened the folder with the contract drafts and handed a copy to Lexington. She tucked a stray tendril of hair behind her ear and pulled the documents toward her then looked directly at him.

"We have some time… I hope…for this." She drew small circles on the papers with the tip of a finger. "It always helps me to envision and plan a project when I understand the genesis of it and the people behind it."

The corner of his mouth curved upward. "I see." He slowly nodded his head. "What would you like to know?"

Everything. "You started to tell me about your brothers earlier. What do they do?"

He chuckled lightly. "Ahh, the Grant brothers. Franklin is the oldest. He's a cardiothoracic surgeon."

"Whoa. Impressive. Here in DC?"

"He practiced here for years. Fell in love with Dina, another surgeon. They got married and moved to Seattle about a year ago."

Their food arrived. They thanked the waiter. Lexington spread the white linen napkin on her lap.

"Then there is Alonzo, celebrity chef to the stars."

"Seriously?" Her brows rose. "That's a real thing?"

"Yep. Travels all over the world. Cooks for movie stars, athletes, politicians, entertainers." He grinned.

"Folks we only read about he has direct lines to in his cell phone."

"Wow." She scooped up a forkful of pasta and scallops. She chewed slowly. "Oh, my goodness. You were right. This is incredible."

Montgomery dug in as well. "Glad you like it."

"Is your globe-hopping brother married as well?"

"Yep. Newlywed. Six months. Mikayla. She's a doll. Crazy how they met. He needed a housekeeper after being away from home for months and she showed up. She was doing it as a side gig and boom—love at first sight. Just what Zo needed in his life."

Lexington watched the animation in his expression when he talked about his brothers and the ring of pride in his voice. Must be nice. All her life she'd longed for a relationship like that with Maxwell. But theirs wasn't a brother/sister love connection. It was more of a competition for their parents' affection and attention. And she always seemed to come up short. Randall, golden child, could do no wrong, no matter how wrong he was; from getting in trouble in school, DUIs, the women, dropping out of three colleges before settling down, the list went on. But he was a natural charmer. Max could convince you that the sky falling was a good thing. For whatever reason, her parents seemed to hold her to some higher, almost unattainable standard until she couldn't take it anymore.

"You okay?"

Lexington blinked Montgomery back into focus. She forced a smile. "Yeah. Fine." She dragged in a breath, pinched her brows together. "Seems as if your brothers met their matrimonial fate on the job."

He chuckled. "You're right." He worked the food on his plate.

"So…what about you?"

He glanced up from beneath his lashes. "Me? What about me?"

Tell me if there is a she in your life. "Why real estate?" she asked instead.

He leaned back a bit, reached for his glass and took a short swallow. "I was always intrigued at construction sites as a kid. I could stand for hours watching these enormous holes get filled day by day until something solid was there," he said, his voice taking on a faraway tone. He leaned forward and linked his fingers on the tabletop. "But as I got older and more aware of what was really happening—the disenfranchisement of families and businesses—I knew I had to change that. I studied real estate law, social sciences and got my law degree."

"Law degree?"

"Yeah, but I don't practice. Just handy. I wanted to put my knowledge and passion into the community where I grew up. All of the property that I rehab or buy is all minority owned and run when the project is complete. This city was built on the backs of our ancestors. The least I can do is offer something to the descendants."

"A developer with heart. A rare commodity in this business."

He looked into her eyes. "Then we need to do our part so it won't stay rare."

In the instant that their gazes connected, she held her breath as his voice dipped to the center of her being, certain that he was going to reach across the table and touch her hand. Instead, he lifted his glass to his lips.

"What about you? Why architecture?"

"I guess, in a way, I was a bit like you growing up. I loved the idea that something you imagined in your head could become real. Something solid that could last for decades—even longer. I was fascinated by the ancient African structures of Egypt—the pyramids are inexplicable, the Greek and Roman temples, basilicas, cathedrals…" She sighed, teased her bottom lip with her teeth. "I was really pretty nerdy as a kid. Always with my head in an art book."

"There's nothing nerdy about you." His dark eyes moved in slow waves across her face. "What could be more intriguing than a woman with brains, beauty and a hunger for…what she loves?"

Her nostrils flared over the sudden pounding in her chest. She started to reach for her glass but didn't dare risk sloshing the contents all over the table and herself. "We should all do what we love, or at the very least enjoy," she managed. "Life is too short."

"Agreed. So, what do you enjoy beyond your work?"

She paused for a moment. "I love to travel, discover exotic places." She held up her finger. "And music." She grinned. "I collect albums. I have quite the collection."

"Really? Any particular genre?"

"That's my problem. I love it all—from the classics to R&B, jazz, blues, hip-hop. You name it."

"A woman after my own heart."

She licked her lip. "What's your pleasure?"

He waited a beat. "Right now for starters."

Her lips parted.

"Where do you stack all those albums? Did you ship them back here?"

She swallowed. "Um, yes. Actually, they're in a storage facility with most of my other things."

He frowned. "Space issue?"

"Something like that. The old saying that you can always come home is true, as long as you don't bring all your stuff with you."

Montgomery laughed. "Are you looking for a place? 'Cause I know a guy," he teased.

"Very funny. Living at home isn't awful. But I suppose if I decide to stay I'm going to have to get a place of my own."

He sat up a bit straighter and reached for his glass. He didn't look at her when he asked, "You're not planning to stay in DC?"

"I'm…not really sure for how long. I know I'll be here for a while—through the end of the project of course."

The waiter stopped at their table. "Can I get you anything else? Refills? Dessert?" he asked while collecting their plates.

"I'm fine. Thank you," Lexington said.

"You can bring the check."

"I'll be right back."

"We never got to talk about the contract," Lexington said.

"Look it over when you get home. I'm available to talk whenever you're ready. But I'm sure you'll find the timeline, the terms and the finances totally acceptable."

She tapped the folder with the tip of her finger. "I'll get back to you by tomorrow. If everything is as reasonable as you say, I'd like to get started as soon as possible."

The waiter returned with the check, took Montgomery's credit card and processed it through the handheld machine.

"Would you go back to Paris?"

She nodded. "I did very well in Europe."

The waiter handed Montgomery his card. "Enjoy the rest of your evening."

Montgomery stood and came around to help Lexington with her coat. "You drove?" he asked, close enough that she felt the gentle warmth of his breath against the back of her neck.

"Yes," she said on a shaken whisper. "I did."

"I was hoping to drive you home, but I'll settle for walking you to your car."

She turned into the halo of his arms around her shoulders.

Neither moved. Neither breathed.

A dish crashed into pieces on the other side of the room, snapping them apart.

Lexington sputtered a laugh. "Guess that's our cue."

"Where are you parked?"

"In the lot across from your building."

He opened the door to the exit. "After you."

"So, I'll hear from you...?"

"Tomorrow, by end of business," Lexington said while she plucked her keys from her purse.

Montgomery took the keys from her hands, pressed the key fob and the locked chirped. He pulled open the driver's side door.

"Thank you," she whispered and slid in behind the wheel. She glanced up at him.

Montgomery leaned down. She held her breath. Her heart banged in her chest.

"Drive safely." He held out her keys.

She ran her tongue along her bottom lip. "Thanks." She stuck the key in the ignition and the engine hummed to life.

"I'm thinking I should follow you home—make sure you arrive safely."

She tipped her head to the side. "Concerned for my safety?" she teased. "Don't think I can take care of myself, Mr. Grant?"

"I have no doubt of what you're capable of. But what kind of gentleman would I be if I let a lady go home alone?"

She sucked on her bottom lip a moment. "Well…if all you're interested in is my 'traveling mercies' as the folks say, it's Albermarle and 16th in case you get lost." She tapped her nail along the steering column. "But if you're interested in a…nightcap, it's a bit crowded. Family."

"Hmm, I think we can work around that. I have plenty of space—and a full bar, if that's cool with you."

She paused a beat. "What's the address in case… I get lost?"

"2100 Murray Street SW. I'll bring my car around." He stepped back and pushed the door shut then walked away.

Lexington dragged in a breath, watched him in her mirrors until he was out of sight. She closed her eyes and realized her heart was racing. Montgomery's face, his lips so close to hers bloomed in front of her. *No more games, Mr. Grant.* She turned on the radio full blast to drown out the rugged sound of his voice and the pounding of her heart. *You want me as bad as I want you.* The corner of her mouth curved upward.

Montgomery's Lexus pulled up alongside her. He lowered his window. "I'm going to take 15th Street."

She gave a nonchalant lift of her chin and put the car in gear. "Lead the way."

Montgomery pulled into his driveway and Lexington pulled in behind him. He turned off the ignition. The next few moves were going to turn this thing in a whole other direction. Was this really what he wanted to do? They could just have a drink, talk for a bit and she could go home. Easy. He'd been down this road before—got involved with someone that he worked with and damn near suffered third-degree burns as a result. This heat was even hotter. But two years out of the frying pan was long enough.

He heard Lexington's car door slam and caught a glimpse of her in his mirror. Yeah, it was worth it. He got out of the car.

"I see you kept up with all my fancy footwork driving."

She laughed. "You'll have to do better than that to lose me—in traffic."

Their gazes challenged each other.

"Hmph. I'll keep that in mind. Come on in." He extended his arm toward the entrance to the house.

He led the way into the sitting area and flipped on the light and adjusted the dimmer, which created more of a mood than illumination.

"Make yourself comfortable. What can I get you to drink?" He walked around the horseshoe-shaped cherry wood bar counter and opened the three-door cabinet to reveal rows of top-shelf liquor, imported wines, sparkling crystal tumblers and wine flutes.

Lexington sauntered over and sat on one of the high-boy stools. "Impressive," she said with a lift of her brow. She placed her purse on the counter. "How good are your mixing skills?"

"Very."

She smiled. "In that case, I'll take a martini." She scanned the shelves. "Make that an apple martini."

"Good choice. Coming right up." He turned to the row of choices. "Belevedere, Grey Goose or Absolut?" He glanced over his shoulder at her.

"Belevedere."

He gave a nod of approval. He took the bottle of vodka and a bottle of sour apple liqueur from the shelf then opened the mini fridge and got some ice.

"Your stock is amazing. Is connoisseur of fine liquors among your résumé talents?"

He smiled. "Actually, it's all due to my brother Alonzo, the chef. He has a drink or specialty wine to go with every meal and occasion and he's always dropping off a bottle of something whenever he's in town. He 'educated' our palates. I had to figure out what to do with it all, so I started practicing, reading up on mixing." He gave a slight shrug. "And here I am."

"You keep surprising me."

He looked at her from under his lashes. "I hope that's a good thing."

"Time will tell."

He paused a beat. "So, Paris. Paris?" he asked with a curious grin.

"Hmm." She laughed lightly. "Paris. Needed to get away. Start new."

He dropped cubes of ice into a sterling silver tumbler, measured the vodka and apple liqueur and shook the contents until the exterior of the shaker glistened from the cold. "That's a pretty long hike to start something new. What about your family business? I would think you'd want to be a part of that—the legacy of it."

He took a strainer from under the counter and poured the contents of the shaker into a delicately stemmed martini glass and placed it in front of Lexington then fixed himself a tumbler of bourbon. He came around and sat next to her.

She spun her stool to face him and lifted her glass. "I'll tell mine if you tell yours."

Montgomery tossed his head back and laughed from deep in his chest. He finally settled his gaze on her and was again totally rocked by the visceral effect she had on him with just a look. His eyes moved slowly across her face. "Deal." He lifted his glass. "You first."

She lowered her head and laughed before taking a sip of her martini. "Hmm."

"Does it meet your approval?"

She placed her glass on the bar top. Her tongue trailed along her bottom lip. "Very much."

"So," he uttered slowly. "Paris."

"It was time for a change. A lot of things ended for me here."

"Oh? Such as?" *Was Gabriel Martin one of them?* "I mean you were part of a successful family business."

She took a sip from her drink. "There was an open international call for a renovation project in Saint-Germain-en-Laye," she said with a perfect French accent. "Things weren't great here for me on a personal level, the family business was more my father and brother's than mine." She sighed and shrugged lightly. "I put in a proposal and was one of five international architects selected. The project was supposed to be for six months, but I extended my work visa—started working on small projects, then bigger ones, made connections and finally set up my own business."

"Now that's what I call impressive."

She smiled. "I had good breaks."

"So…wait you have your own business in Paris—what's happening with it while you're here?"

"I have two great assistants who are holding things down."

"Until you go back." It was as much of a statement as a question.

She responded by finishing her drink and glancing off. "My father always believed that the business should be handed down to the son. Clearly I don't fit the bill."

They both sputtered laughter.

"That bad huh?" He finished his drink.

"When the opportunity presented itself I took it."

"So, when this job is over, there's really nothing holding you here. You have a whole life on the other side of the globe."

She slipped from the stool and stood in front of him. "But I'm here now."

Montgomery slowly rose, looked into the eyes turned up to his. This was the last exit before no return. He lightly traced her jaw with the tip of his finger and watched her breath hitch and her lashes flutter.

"I'm going to kiss you," he rasped.

Lexington draped her arms around his shoulders and cupped the back of his head in her palm. "Not if I kiss you first," she whispered before tasting him.

He knew when he kissed her that it would be special, but not this—this heat, this spinning thing in his gut, this thump in his veins. He parted her lips with a swipe of his tongue and savored the taste of her mixed with the sweetness of the martini. Her moan fluttered in his belly. He looped his arm around her waist and pulled her tight against him.

She lifted up and rocked her pelvis against his blooming erection. He felt his knees give and cupped her derriere, tugged her tight. Tearing his mouth away from hers, he dragged his lips along the cords of her throat, nibbling and licking the sweet, soft skin until she began to whimper and quake in his embrace.

His mouth drifted down to the deep neckline of the silky white blouse. Her fingertips dug into his arms. Her breasts heaved with a sudden intake of air, offering them up as if in invitation, and he accepted.

Lexington moaned as his lips and tongue took advantage of the invitation. He cupped her breasts and was stunned to realize that there was nothing between them except her blouse. He dipped his hand into the valley of her blouse and caressed the perfect bare mounds, teasing the dark nipples until they rose and hardened, waiting to be suckled.

She unfastened the button at her waist that held her

blouse closed. Montgomery eased back. He looked into her eyes then downward as she slowly parted her blouse. His breath caught in his throat.

"God, you're…incredible."

The silky white fabric drifted to the floor.

"Touch me," she whispered.

"Is that all you want?" He placed kisses in the deep valley of her breasts.

"It's just the beginning," she said on a sigh as her head lolled back giving him full access.

"Yes, it is," he groaned and sucked the tip of her nipple between his lips.

Lexington's cry was music and he rode it, from right to left, down to the concave of her stomach. He lifted the hem of her little black skirt, found the elastic of her panties that she wiggled out of. He played with the soft hair on her mound, slid a finger along the slick slit.

"Ohhh."

Montgomery eased her down to the stool. She sat and languidly spread her thighs for him, and he played until the slick skin glistened, and the tiny pearl hardened and throbbed, begging for release and her cries rose to a crescendo that neither could ignore.

"Let's go. Not here," he ground out. He took her hand and led her to his upstairs bedroom.

Hands and mouths found every inch of exposed skin.

Montgomery tugged off his shirt, tossed it to the floor. Lexington loosened his belt and unzipped him. His erection poked through the slit in his shorts. She dipped inside and wrapped her fingers around him, kneaded and stroked him. He groaned in pleasure and hiked her skirt up over her hips and walked her back toward his bed.

She tumbled down onto the king-size mattress and Montgomery followed, pinning her beneath him.

Montgomery cupped her cheeks in his palms and looked deep into her eyes, searching for any hint of hesitation. He found nothing but desire in her gaze. Tenderly he kissed her, long and deep, needing to slow everything down and savor these first moments. He wanted their loving to make a difference.

It had been so long since she'd been with a man. Was this pure attraction or long overdue desire? But when he touched her, kissed her, held her the questions and any doubt that swirled didn't matter. Nothing mattered but what he was doing to her body—awakening it again.

"Ohhh, yesss." She was on fire. The blood that coursed through her veins was lit with lust. She didn't just want him adoring the outside of her she wanted to feel him inside of her, put to rest the imagining that taunted her from the moment she met Montgomery Grant. And if what he was doing to her body was a prelude of what else he had to give her, she was more than ready to give as good as she got.

He spread her thighs, draped her knees over his shoulders and blessed her with short flicks of his tongue.

She gripped the sheets into her fists as her hips rose and fell of their own volition against his expert mouth. He was good at this. Damn good. She didn't want it to stop, but she needed it to or she would come. Hard. And she wasn't ready. Not… "Ohhhh, god. Ahhhh." If he wasn't gripping her hips she would have flown off the bed right up to the ceiling. Wave after wave crashed through her until she was weak and nearly sobbing in ecstasy.

Her chest heaved as she gulped in air. Montgomery did a slow crawl up her body, planting kisses along the way. He reached over and opened the nightstand drawer, felt around for a condom packet and held it up.

"You want to do the honors?"

She thrilled at his devilishly sexy grin. "It's the least I could do." She took the packet and tore it open with her teeth.

Montgomery rose up on his knees, his rock-hard erection at her command. She licked her lips and by taunting increments rolled the condom down the length of his shaft.

"How'd I do?" she whispered.

"Let's find out."

Before she could react he'd flipped her onto her stomach, grabbed a pillow and shoved it under her hips so that she was lifted to accept him. He ran his finger down the length of her spine. She shivered. Moaned. He gripped her hips. He pressed up against her wet opening. She gasped. He pushed into the slick heat of her. The sensation shot through him and into the air.

"Ahhhh, damn. Oh." He began to move in and out of her, diving as deep as space and gravity would allow.

"Yesss," she cried and rocked her rear against him.

His head spun. He needed to look her in her eyes when he came. He pulled out. Lexington gasped.

"Turn over," he ordered.

She turned onto her back.

Tenderly he brushed the hair away from her face,

leaned down and kissed her softly on the lips, then with more urgency.

She bent her knees. Montgomery groaned. She reached for him between her thighs. "I need you back where you were," she said on a breath.

"Whatever the lady wants."

Their moans and sighs mixed and mingled, rose and fell as limbs entwined and they tried to move beyond the merging of their bodies to unite their souls. Slick skin slapped faster, harder...

"Look at me," he ground out.

Lexington's eyes fluttered open.

"This is what I've been waiting to give you." He thrust swift and deep within her.

The climax hit her so hard that her limbs stiffened, her body arched as if electrified. She tried to cry out but the sound hung in her throat. The sensations rolled up from the balls of her feet and imploded. All she could do was hold on to heaven, and he went with her, the grip and release of her tight walls sending him hurtling over the edge.

Montgomery's body slumped with a groan onto Lexington. Their hearts pounded so hard and fast that the bed still vibrated. He lifted her damp hair away from the side of her face with the tip of his finger and tenderly kissed her neck. Lexington sighed softly. Montgomery rolled onto his back then turned on his side to face her.

How did he wind up right where he didn't—or at least shouldn't—want to be? *You know why. Lexington Randall struck a match in you the moment you set eyes on her.* Simple. But now what? The last thing he needed was any kind of complication when business gets all twisted up with a sexual roll in the sack. Was that what was happening?

He watched the slow rise and fall of her breasts, the way her large dark nipples peaked and pointed upward. He felt the stir between his thighs. She moaned softly then turned toward him. Her eyes looked dreamy, her skin glistened.

"Hey," she whispered as if slowly rising from a peaceful sleep.

He stroked her hip and kissed the curve of her shoulder. "Get you anything?"

She dragged in a deep breath. Her eyes danced over his face. She cupped his cheek in her palm. "Well…that was definitely the main course…" She slid her hand down to his rising erection. "I'm ready for dessert." She wrapped her fingers around him.

He bit down on his bottom lip as his lashes lowered and he sucked in air from between his teeth.

Lexington stroked him up and down, slow and firm, until he was stiff and throbbing in her palm. Somehow he managed to grab another rubber from the nightstand. While she was busy, turning him up, he tore the packet open. Lexington stopped, looked him in the eye with a light of pure seduction gleaming there, took the condom from him and rolled it along his length.

"I think I want to see what it's like when you're no longer in control," she said before straddling him and taking them on a long, leisurely ride to ecstasy.

"I should get going," she whispered into the room lit by moonlight. "It's nearly one."

Montgomery moaned his way out of a half sleep. He draped his leg across her thighs. "Don't think so," he mumbled into her ear. "Need to show you my breakfast skills."

She giggled and snuggled closer. "Anything like your bedroom skills?"

He let his fingers trail along the rise of her breasts. "I'll let you decide," he grumbled low in his throat before taking a nipple between his lips.

Lexington sat at the kitchen counter, draped in Montgomery's shirt from the night before. *So cliché.* Over the rim of her coffee mug, she eyed his muscled thighs exposed in a pair of black boxers while he fried bacon in a cast iron pan. This first morning after seemed so meant-to-be. Easy. *Sip.* He had great legs for a guy, strong thighs—great body in general. Every inch of him was taut muscle—the broad back and chest, rippling abs and long arms, and his… She sighed and took another sip. So now what? They'd "done it," and done it damned good, too. Did it mean that they were in some kind of relationship, and if so what kind? Did he expect things from her? What did she expect from him? This is how stuff got messy. This was a job, nothing more and when it was done and she got her father's business straightened out she was going back to Paris.

She cleared her throat. "I should probably review that contract. I did promise to get back to you by end of business."

Montgomery glanced at her from over his shoulder. His eyes cinched in the corners. "You okay?"

"Yeah, fine." Her brows lifted to punctuate her words.

He studied her for a moment. "If you're sure." He turned back to the stove. "Pretty certain you left the envelope in your car." He turned fully around. "I wouldn't go out there like *that* though." A wickedly sexy grin slid like sunrise across his mouth.

The heat rose from the soles of her feet and moved around in the pit of her stomach. She shifted her butt in the chair and crossed her legs. "That's probably true."

"People might talk." He chuckled. "I have a reputation to uphold."

She cupped her palms around the mug. "So…are you saying you don't have a stream of women coming in and out at all hours?"

"Pretty much." He turned back to the stove, removed the bacon from the pan and placed the strips on a plate. He prepped a second skillet for the frittata.

Don't do it, Lexi. Don't… "No one special, huh?" Inwardly she cringed. No way to snatch the words back. *He probably thinks I'm some psycho stalker.* She watched the muscles in his back flex.

"No. Can't say that there is. Hasn't been for a while, actually." He turned slowly toward her. "What about you?"

She swallowed. "Well, to be honest…a while ago, a long while ago I was involved with Gabriel Martin. I understand he works for you." There. Done.

He leaned against the fridge. "Yeah, he mentioned something about that. Apparently he saw you the day you came to the site."

She dragged in a breath and raised the cup to her mouth.

"Is that going to be a problem?"

Her gaze flew to his. "No. Absolutely not. That was a long time ago." She flicked her hand in dismissal.

He seemed to be testing if her claim would hold up under the weight of his gaze. Finally, he gave a light shrug and turned back to the stove.

"Cool."

The knot in her stomach loosened. But why the hell did it matter what he thought anyway? This was just a thing between them. A temporary thing.

"I'll let you know if I have any questions about the contract," she said, standing next to her car.

"Not a problem. I'm sure it will meet your approval."

She opened the car door. "I'll call you."

He grinned and placed his hand on her shoulder. "That's my line."

There was that look again that got her all mushy in the head. "Then say it," she managed to whisper.

He leaned in and covered her mouth with his, taking his time as if needing to commit the moment to memory. Slowly he eased back. "I'll call you."

Lexington gave him a tight-lipped grin. "Have a great day, Mr. Grant," she teased and slid in behind the wheel.

He shut her door and stepped back while she pulled out of the driveway and was gone.

Montgomery flopped down on his couch, stretched his long legs out in front of him and leaned his head back. She'd been gone only a few hours but it felt longer. He should have made that kiss last, then convinced her to spend the day in bed with him. He was pretty sure that she would have let him. But then what? Was that the road he really wanted to go down—getting *that* involved with someone he was working with? He'd already broken all of his rules. A smile creased his cheeks. It was hella worth it.

His cell phone vibrated on his hip. He raised up and pulled the phone from his pocket. Frowned at the number he didn't recognize.

"Hello?"

"Hey…"

A shockwave of recognition passed through him. "Stella." He sat up.

"Hey, Monty."

"How are you?"

"I'm good. No complaints. I'm sure you weren't expecting to hear from me."

"Can't say that I was."

"I'm in town."

"Really?"

"Since last week."

"Oh. For work? How long are you staying?" He crossed his ankle over his knee, and squeezed the phone in a death grip.

She paused. "Actually, I moved back."

His foot dropped to the floor. "Moved back?"

"I know." She sputtered a laugh. "I didn't think it would happen."

He didn't think a lot of things would happen, especially between him and Stella; like falling in love with her, making plans with her and her walking away from it all with barely an explanation. Two years seemed long enough to get over Stella Vincent until he'd heard her voice again and all the ugliness roared back. His temple began to pound.

"I was hoping maybe we could get together for lunch or maybe tonight for a drink—talk."

"Talk?" He laughed but it wasn't funny. "After all this time, Stella. About what exactly?" The last thing he needed to ever do was meet her at night for drinks. Nonstarter.

"You have every reason not to ever want to see or speak to me again, but I owe you an explanation Monty."

"Do you, now?"

"Please," she whispered. "I really want to see you."

A million reasons why not ran through his head. Revisiting the past only worked in the art world. Yet, there was that space he'd dug out inside of himself where he'd buried the memories of what they once were, now those memories clawed to be unearthed.

Even as he agreed he knew it was the wrong decision.

Just as he was walking out the door, Sterling called wanting an update on the meeting with Lexington and if he planned to come in to the office. He put the cell phone on speaker.

"I'll tell you all about it a little later. I gave her the draft of the contracts. She's going to review everything and confirm before end of business. I don't see a problem."

"Okay, brother. You sound rushed. I catch you at a bad time?"

"Uh, no. I was heading out."

"Hot date?" he teased.

"No." He cleared his throat, checked his pocket for his keys and shut the door behind him. "I'm meeting Stella. For a late lunch."

"Stella? Stella-up-and-disappeared-without-a-word Stella? That Stella?"

Montgomery unlocked his car, tossed his jacket on the passenger seat.

"When did she get back?"

"She said a week ago." He got in and turned the key in the ignition. "Moved back, apparently." He secured the phone in the holder.

"Whoa! Stella moved back after ghosting you two years ago and you're going to meet her for lunch? Am I gonna wind up seeing you on one of those *Lifetime* movies when the guy kills the ex and starts a new life?"

"First of all, when do you watch *Lifetime*? And second, it's always the woman who's the killer." He eased out of the driveway.

"Oh…and *you* would know that how?"

Montgomery snickered. "Everybody knows that. Look, we'll talk later."

"I think you need a wingman. You know how you are about Stella."

"Was. Was. She's past tense. Rearview. She said she wants to explain. That's it."

"Oh, sure."

He laughed. "Sterling, I got this, man. Chill."

"Yeah, okay. Just stay focused."

"Plan to. Later, cuz."

"Later."

Montgomery turned on the radio to the local jazz station in the hopes of doing what he told his cousin to do, *chill*. It was only lunch. Nothing more. Whatever went down between him and Stella was two years and counting in the past. He wasn't even sure if an explanation mattered at this point. But there was that tick of human instinct that needed to know why—get closure, and then maybe he could move beyond simple physical attraction to a woman to something more meaningful. Stella did a number on him. He had to admit that, but at some point he had to let it go—for real. Maybe today was finally the day.

Twice, he drove around the block of SpeakEasy, the blues and jazz lounge in Georgetown, before finally finding a parking spot. For a couple of minutes he sat behind the wheel moving one scenario after the other through his head: how would she look, what would she say, would he still feel the same when he actually saw her again, will any of this matter? He hit the steering wheel with the heel of his palm, snatched the keys from the ignition and got out.

Montgomery pulled open the door to the lounge and was immediately enveloped in the embrace of Blackness, from the artwork of Basquiat, Lawrence, Catlett, and Kara Walker, the iconic photography of Gordon Parks and Carrie Mae Weems, to the free library that took up a full wall from floor to ceiling of Morrison, Dubois, Walker, Gaines, McMillan, McFadden, Jenkins, Alers, Wilkerson, and Adichie. Faces of some of the great blues and jazz entertainers dotted the tables as centerpieces and made for great conversation trivia.

SpeakEasy was a living, breathing piece of Black art and had some of the best food in the District.

"Welcome to SpeakEasy. Table or would you like to sit at the bar?"

"Um," he peered over the hostess's head. "I'm actually meeting some—"

"Monty."

He turned toward the voice coming from behind him. A knot of air lodged in his chest. Seeing her again—raw. Everything about her was as he remembered. Maybe her hair was a bit longer and there seemed to be an air of calm assurance that wafted around her even in the middle of whatever this was between them.

"Hey." He forced a half smile and slung his hands into his pockets.

She leaned up and kissed his cheek, stared into his eyes until he could feel her touch his soul. The familiar scent of her drifted around him.

"Sorry I'm late. Parking is still crazy around here." Her butterfly-winged laughter fluttered along with notes of Miles Davis's trumpet that played in the background.

"Some things never change."

She glanced away, tucked her shoulder length hair behind her left ear exposing the tiny heart-shaped tattoo that she'd gotten on a dare early in their relationship.

Montgomery cleared his throat then turned back to the hostess. "A table would be great."

She plucked two menus from the holder. "Follow me."

Montgomery maneuvered Stella in front of him and they followed the hostess around the circular tables and stage.

She seated them at a table near the back by a window facing K Street and the waterfront. "Your waiter will be with you shortly. Can I get you something to drink?" She glanced from one to the other.

"A mimosa might be nice," Stella said then looked to Montgomery.

Montgomery unbuttoned his jacket. "Hennessey, neat."

"Coming right up."

Montgomery dragged in a breath and slowly exhaled. He leaned back against the cushion of his seat and glanced at Stella from beneath his lashes. "So, I'm here. Talk. You apparently had good reason to leave DC," he swallowed down *and me*. "Why come back?"

Stella tucked in her lips and linked her fingers together on top of the table. She blinked several times. "I know what I did was wrong, Monty," she began softly. "But I didn't have a choice."

"What the hell are you talking about—you didn't have a choice?" He leaned in, his voice low, his expression simultaneously taut and creased. "We were together. Us. You and I. We had plans. One day I wake up and you're fucking gone," he hissed. "Gone!"

Her chest heaved.

The waiter returned with their drinks.

Montgomery withdrew, looked everywhere but at Stella.

"Can I take your orders?"

"Give us a minute," Montgomery managed. He turned the burn of his full attention on Stella. The rage, the hurt and betrayal that he'd spent months beating down had roared back with a ferociousness that shook him. He reached for his tumbler and tossed back his drink in nearly one long swallow. His eyes squeezed shut as the heat of the alcohol slid down his throat. Finally, he focused on Stella. "You just left one day. No warning. Nothing but a letter in the mail. *I'm sorry, but it's over*," he said, suddenly sounding as weary as the situation had become.

She reached across the table to cover his balled fist, but he eased his hand away. "I was sick… I found out I was sick…after I found out I was pregnant."

His stomach dropped. "What?" He leaned closer. "What are you telling me?" His eyes scoured her expression.

She took a sip of her mimosa. "You remember that I hadn't been feeling well, the last couple of months…"

"You kept telling me you were just working too hard, traveling for work was taking a toll…" he said, the frustration apparent in his tone.

"I saw a specialist while I was in New York, and after a battery of tests I was diagnosed with lupus." She paused. "And I was six weeks pregnant."

His lips parted but no words came out.

"The immunologist put me on medication to ease and hopefully control the symptoms, but he warned me that the pregnancy would only escalate them. The physical pain during the flare-ups was already unbearable." She tugged in a breath. "Going through with it would have…could have killed me."

He struggled to make sense of what she was telling him. The words were jumbled like a box of puzzle pieces, all mixed up.

"I wasn't… I couldn't go through with the pregnancy." She pressed her polished lips into a tight line and curled and uncurled her fingers.

His gaze drifted from Stella to the table, to the other diners, couples strolling past the window to nothing at all. Finally, he looked at her. "You could have told me," he muttered, his voice sounding foreign to his ears. "You *should* have told me. We could have worked it out, Stella. I deserved to know." He swallowed over the ache in his throat. "About…everything."

"I'm sorry." The brown of her eyes glistened and filled. Her lashes fluttered as she fought back tears. She snatched up the napkin and dabbed at her eyes. Her voice cracked. "I'm sorry." She swallowed. "I knew how much you wanted a family one day, and your career and business were taking off. You wanted to finally settle down." She sniffed. Her nostrils flared. "I couldn't do that to you. I wouldn't."

Montgomery stared at her as if seeing her for the first time. *A child.* He'd had one version of what their life could have been and she had another. At some point she'd stopped trusting him to love her unconditionally. He would have stood by her. He believed that deep in his soul, and they would have gotten through it together. *A child.* He wanted to understand how they could have gotten to this place from where they once were.

"So…how are you—with the illness…with every-thing?"

Stella drew in a long breath. Her forced smile wob-bled. "I have good days and bad. More good over the past six months or so. They finally figured out the right combination of meds and diet that work for me."

Montgomery slowly nodded. "That's good. I'm glad… The preg—the baby…you were okay?"

Her gaze dropped downward. Montgomery reached across the table and covered her hand with his.

She lifted her head to look at him. "It was the hardest thing I've ever done in my life, Monty." Her voice broke into tiny pieces and scattered across the table. "There's not a day that goes by that I don't think about it."

He squeezed her hand. There was no need to say the words; that he would have understood her decision, that he would have stood with her through her illness. No reason to revisit the past.

Stella pulled in a breath, sniffed back her tears. "So that's why I left."

He pursed his lips and nodded slowly as if he could ever fully understand. "Okay. That's why you left, but now you're back—and beyond this mega revelation, why are you here to stay?"

"A great job offer, actually. I'll be working for WJLA television."

His brows lifted in admiration. "Niiiice. Congrats."

She genuinely smiled for the first time. "I'm excited. Steady work. No more traveling, great benefits."

"When do you start?"

"Two weeks." She leaned forward. "I know this may be an imposition, but I was hoping you could find me a place to live. I'm looking for a small house—to rent with the option to buy—or a condo, anywhere in the DMV area. The station is putting me up at a really great Airbnb, but that runs out at the end of next month, and I'd like to get something of my own before then."

"Tall order. Short time frame." He signaled the

waiter. "I'll have another," he said, holding up his glass. He focused on Stella. "Another?"

"No." She smiled at her half-full flute. "One is my limit. But I'd love to share a plate of hot wings," she said to the waiter then turned her focus on Montgomery "—like we used to."

The waiter left to fill their orders.

He wasn't going down that rabbit hole of "like we used to" yesteryear. "I'll see what I can do about finding you something. I'm sure there are plenty of properties that would suit you."

The waiter returned with Montgomery's drink. "Wings are on the way."

Montgomery raised his glass. "Welcome back to DC," he said with as much enthusiasm as he could muster, still shaken by her revelations.

Stella touched her glass to his. "Thanks."

"Where'd you park?" Montgomery asked as he held the door for her to exit.

"On the next block."

"I'll walk you to your car."

"It's fine. I really appreciate you even coming here." She pressed her hand to his chest. "It was good to see you, Monty."

"I'll, uh, start looking for you. Let you know as soon as I find some choices."

She tucked in her lips and nodded. "Thanks. Well," she said on a breath. "Goodbye." She turned and walked away.

He watched her until she blended in with the late afternoon strollers before walking to his car.

On the drive home Montgomery replayed the events of his day. It had spun completely off its axis. He'd been trying to get his mind right about Lexington Randall and what working with her would entail. It was clear as crystal that there was something steaming between them and they'd proven that last night and into the morning. Something that he was totally unprepared for. Then here comes a blast from the past, Stella Vincent no less. Now his head was on the spin cycle. Too much to process. What he needed was a stiff drink and some quiet time. He'd told Sterling he'd be in the office at some point, but that wasn't happening. Maybe things would make more sense on the other side of this day. Like his mother's favorite refrain, *joy comes in the morning.* He sighed. That was the most he could hope for. The least was some clarity on what the hell he was going to do next because clearly he was in free fall mode.

He stopped at a red light. The time on the dash clock read four fifteen. He hadn't heard from Lexington. At least not directly. Maybe she'd called the office. What if she changed her mind? *Stella.* Damn, how would he ever wrap his mind around what could have been? If he thought he was hard-pressed to forgive and forget that she'd torpedoed their relationship with no warning, this was on an entirely different level. A flash of him as a father dashed for an instant across his line of sight. One thought tumbled over the other.

The blare of a car horn snapped him to attention. The light had turned green. He drove across the intersection with the intention of heading home. He tapped an icon on the dash. "Call Sterling."

The phone rang through the speakers.

"Hey, bruh. Where are you? Thought you were coming in today."

"Yeah. So did I. Look, you heading home now or you have plans?"

"Nothing special. Was gonna head out in about fifteen minutes or so. What's up? It's Stella, ain't it? I told you that you needed a wingman."

"You mighta been right. Need to talk."

"Not a problem. Wanna swing by my place or meet up somewhere?"

"I can come by you. Not really up for a bunch of people."

"Damn, sounds serious. I can be home in like forty-five minutes."

"Cool. Thanks, man. See you in a few."

"Oh, yeah, we got the go-ahead from Randall Architect and Design. They have no changes to the contract."

His stomach clenched. She did call...but not him. *Keeping it professional?*

"You still there?"

"Yeah, yeah, sorry...crazy traffic. Listen ask Cherise to get the final version out to Randall Architect and Design for signatures, will ya?"

"Sure. Not a problem."

"Later."

"Use your key if you get there before me."

"Will do." He disconnected the call.

He made the turn onto Sixteenth Street, drove past the White House and grumbled under his breath but was momentarily emboldened as he drove along the BLM mural that dominated the street, a stark reminder of the reckoning the nation was grappling with.

Since he had some time he decided to make a pit stop at his place to pick up a bottle of Hennessy and a change of clothes. He had a feeling it was going to be a long night.

Five

Lexi sat at her desk near the window shifting her gaze between the rising moon above the hodgepodge rows of framed brick and shingled single-family homes that dotted inner-city DC, and the new sketches on her computer screen. Unable to concentrate she closed the cover of her laptop. Montgomery clouded her thoughts. Naïvely she'd harbored the ridiculous notion that they'd tumble around in bed, have knockout sex and magically that thing she'd felt for him would simply go away. Or at the very least the burning embers would be reduced to smoldering ashes. She couldn't have been more wrong.

Simply put, Montgomery Grant was amazing. He was sexy as all hell, smart, funny, a beast in bed, could make a dynamite martini and fry up some bacon in a pan to boot. She grinned at the television reference. What she really needed right now was a girls' night out to dish and whoop and holler and share the awesomeness of Montgomery. Humph. First, she needed some girlfriends.

She pushed up from the desk with a sigh, realizing in that instant just how alone she was. She slid her feet into a pair of red flip-flops and went downstairs, fixed a glass of rum and Coke and went to sit on the back porch.

A light breeze unsettled the leaves on the towering oak tree that shaded the entire backyard. Like the leaves her thoughts swayed to and fro. At times like this she would spill her heart and soul out to her best friend, Michelle. Her insides twisted. Even after all this time, her betrayal still hurt her deeply.

She and Michelle had been best friends since the first day of their freshman year in high school. One of those crazy fate things brought them together when they were running for the bus and the driver shut the door and pulled off. Up to that moment she didn't think anyone could cuss more than she did until she met Michelle Porter, who went off on a three-minute takedown of the bus driver and every oppressor since 1619. She predated Shuri from *Black Panther* in labeling them all "colonizers."

At the time she didn't know whether to be alarmed or amused with the boisterous girl. Her saffron cheeks were flushed with fury as she cussed and paced, and in the moment, Lexington experienced firsthand a human storm as lightning could easily flash from her green eyes.

"Here comes another one," she'd managed to get in between the rant.

Michelle blinked those green eyes at her as if seeing her for the first time. "Damn, you must think I'm nuts."

"Not at all. Not really."

"Just ain't right, you know. They can't just do us any old kinda way."

"I hear ya."

The bus pulled to a stop, the door opened and just like a light switch that had been flipped Michelle turned sweet as sugar, greeting the bus driver and the passengers until finding a seat in the back. It was amazing to witness and kind of unsettling that one person could go from zero to three hundred in the blink of an eye.

"Here's two seats. You want the window or the aisle?"

And it never occurred to her that maybe I didn't want to sit with her but I did anyway. "Aisle is cool," is what she thought she'd said. It wouldn't be the first time that she'd just gone along with Michelle. But from that first day up until four years ago, they were tighter than sisters by blood, even if they were like night and day. Where Michelle was outright in your face rebellious, she took the opposite stance—thought things through, weighed all the options and outcomes. Michelle simply wanted to go for it and screw the consequences.

Lexi took a slow sip of her drink and stretched her legs out in front of her. It seemed like forever ago or maybe only yesterday, but it still hurt. No matter how many times she trampled through the ugliness that happened the only thing she came away with was that it was classic Michelle. It could be ironically funny but it wasn't. Michelle saw something she wanted—Gabriel—and like she always did she went after what she wanted.

It didn't matter to her how she got him or what irreparable damage it would cause.

There were lessons buried in the rubble; never let down your guard, keep your enemies close and don't open your heart. Lessons that she'd reshaped her life and spirit to live by—until Monty. She needed to get her barriers back up, shore up her emotions and keep her eyes on the prize. The upside she supposed was that however things went down between her and Monty, she didn't have some other "frenemy" to contend with.

She finished her drink and set it down on the off-white plastic table, just as her father opened the screen door and stepped outside.

"Didn't know you were out here," he said, the warm smile illuminated in the waning light.

"Yeah. I forgot how nice it was back here."

He took a seat next to her in the lounge chair. "Hmm, your mother and I spent many a night back here talking… planning." He chuckled softly, slowly shook his head with the memory. "Your mother always had some grand plan—if it wasn't redoing the house, it was campaigning for the latest community cause, or how we could get Max to focus on his school work so he could make something of himself, and what kind of young man would be acceptable for you with all of your energy and intelligence." He shot his daughter a loving gaze.

Lexington shifted in her seat to better look at her father.

"Was having a man the only goal that you and mom saw for me?"

"Lexi, that's not what I meant. Of course we wanted more than that for you, sweetheart."

She pushed out a deep sigh and spoke softly. "Never seemed that way. No matter what ridiculous thing Max did, no matter how awful he was at picking up the mantel of the business, you never saw *me*. Not really. There was that old-school part of you that could only imagine your son—no matter how incapable—of walking in your shoes. I guess simply naming me after you was sufficient. At least Mom encouraged me to go after my dreams in a mainly man's world because she knew it was what I wanted and that I was good."

Lexington Sr., lowered his head. "I made a lot of mistakes when it came to you and your brother and this business. I'm sorry, Lexi. I didn't want to see what was right in front of me. Now the chickens have come home to roost."

"I'll do what I can, because I believe in all of the amazing work you've done over the years, and the importance of a business like ours remaining a part of this community." She paused. "I got the contract, Dad. I'll be the architect for Essex House. I'll do what I can to make Randall Architect and Design solvent…and then I'm going back to Paris." She pushed to her feet and looked down into her father's upturned face. "Apology accepted." She pulled open the screen door then stopped. "Gabriel is the project manager." She sputtered a laugh of disbelief. "But I'm not going to let that get in the way. However, don't you dare let him through the front door if he comes here."

"Figured I'd throw some steaks on the grill, roast some corn on the cob. Cool?" Sterling said as he and Montgomery shared a beer in the kitchen.

"Sounds good." He hopped up on the stool while Sterling took two steaks out of the fridge and a bag of corn on the cob.

"Got any of Alonzo's special sauce left from the last time he was in town?"

Sterling turned toward his cousin, with a bottle of sauce held up in his hand. "And ya know that." He grinned. "Wouldn't be caught without it. When's he coming back?"

"Your guess is as good as mine. He's still in Ghana. It was only supposed to be for two weeks, but it's a month already."

"What about Mikayla? Did she go too?" He lightly pounded the steaks with a small mallet.

Montgomery smirked. "You know those two are locked at the hip. Mikayla has her business running well enough that she can leave it in the hands of her staff and she'll hop on a plane in a minute."

They both laughed.

Sterling raised his bottle of beer. "Somebody's gotta live that life."

Montgomery clinked his bottle with Sterling's. "Got that right." He took a swallow. "You know that my brothers and I, and you, the four of us were hell-bent and determined not to let a relationship overshadow our careers. We didn't have time for that."

"Yeah. And it looks like the Grant brothers are falling like dominos, cuz. I'm gonna be the last man standing." His shoulders shook with laughter.

Montgomery rested his elbows on the counter. "Very funny. Anyway, whatcha trying to say?"

Sterling took the two steaks and put them on a platter. He turned to his cousin. "I'm sayin' you have been sprung my good brother. But what I want to know is what are you going to do about it, and what is Stella's story?" He started toward the back porch. "Grab the corn for me and the cooler."

Sterling closed the lid to the propane grill, and much like everything else in Sterling's home and life it was impressive to say the least. The grill cost him almost as much as a used car, but it was a beaut. Double racks, temperature controls, drawers and cabinets underneath—the works. And it grilled up the best steaks this side of the Mississippi. Of course it came with Alonzo's seal of approval.

"So, what happened?"

Montgomery leaned back in the striped lounge chair and crossed his feet at the ankles. He finished off his beer and reached for another in the cooler that rested between the two chairs.

"Well I did what I told myself I would never do—again—get involved with someone I work with." He slowly shook his head in wonder and a smile slid across his face. "But brother…it was worth it. Damn! It was worth it."

Sterling tossed his head back and laughed, then pointed his bottle at his cousin. "Told you. Told you, you were sprung."

Montgomery's brows drew tight. "Yeah, I only wish that I could honestly say it was only about the sex."

"Oh, boy." He pushed up from his seat and went to check the food. The mouthwatering aroma of sizzling steaks coated in Alonzo's special sauce wafted in the air. He flipped them over and used the basting brush to cover the up side with sauce. "So it's clearly more than letting off some steam. You got a real thing for her."

"Yeah, man. I do. I wanted to pass it off as just a physical attraction, but it's more than that. She's funny, and smart as hell, well traveled, talented."

"Sounds like the whole package. I hear a 'but' in there somewhere."

"But she plans to return to Paris when this job is over and she never gave me any real indication that she wants to take it any further than where it is right now."

Sterling shrugged. "I don't see the problem. You don't really want to make this a real thing, she's not staying—problem solved."

Montgomery looked off into the distance. "Yeah, I guess so."

"Sounds like we might need to break out that bottle of Hennessy you brought over." Sterling went back into the house to get it, returned with the bottle and two glasses. "I take it just letting it be a 'thing' is not really what you want."

Montgomery turned his body toward his cousin. "Man, I thought I was good. But when she said she planned to go back to Paris—it really threw me." He frowned and went on to tell Sterling about Lexington's business in Paris, and the parts that she revealed about her family dynamics that led to her leaving.

Sterling opened the top to the grill and took off the steaks, opened the bottom rack and took off the four ears of corn and put everything on a large platter. "Come on now, I don't do serving. So help yourself."

Montgomery grinned. "One of these days it would be nice to be treated like a guest."

"Ha! *One of these days* are the magic words."

The cousins loaded their plates and set up at the rectangular wood table beneath the awning.

"Seems like the 'Ms. Randall' issue is not going to resolve itself until you decide just how much time and energy you want to invest in a relationship that you know is only temporary."

"Yeah. You're right." He cut a piece of steak and popped it in his mouth. His lids slowly closed and he moaned with pleasure. "Hmm, damn is it the steak or the sauce?"

"Both. I got skills with the grill, but the sauce is the truth."

They chuckled.

Montgomery opened the bottle of Hennessy and poured for them both. "And then there's Stella."

"Yeah," Sterling said on a breath. "What is she doing here and what does she want with you?"

Montgomery took a short sip of his drink, let the warmth slide down his throat and settle in his stomach. "So, anyway she asks to meet me…" He went on to recount the conversation and the bombshells.

"Daaamn, man. I—" he shook his head. "I don't even know what to tell you bro. I'm sorry."

Montgomery rocked his jaw, took another swallow of his drink and dug into his steak. He chewed thoughtfully. "Really messed my head up, ya know."

"I hear ya. So now what? She's gonna stay, you know why she left…that change anything?"

"That's what I've been struggling with since I left Stella."

"But what is she saying? Is she looking to pick up where y'all left off, just put the past in the rearview like nothing happened?" he asked, becoming more incredulous by the minute.

Montgomery shook his head. "I don't know and I didn't press the point. She's going to start her new job." He cleared his throat and looked across the table at his cousin. "She asked me to help her find a place."

Sterling's head popped up from looking down at his plate. "Say what? I know you told her no."

Montgomery cleared his throat. "Not exactly."

Sterling leaned forward. "Look, Stella did a real number on you. I get it. Since she up and left you've made it a point to keep the brakes on with women. I get it. Now you finally run into someone that put the spark back and bam here comes Stella with an explanation." He shook his head. "Bottom line is going backward is never a good look. Don't even get that in your head." He stabbed a piece of steak with his fork and waved it at his cousin. "I don't care what her story is. What's to say she won't hide something else from you or up and disappear again?"

"Yeah, I know."

"As for Lexington, I say easy does it. See where it goes. The project is going to take six months at least. Besides, if it turns into something, Paris is a pretty damned good place to travel to."

Montgomery's mouth formed a lopsided grin. "Yeah, how 'bout that." He paused a beat. "I'm going to get one of the members from the real estate staff to help Stella with finding a place."

"Exactly." He pointed his fork at Montgomery. "That way she'll be clear about what the deal is. No confusion or mixed signals."

Montgomery leaned back and sipped his drink. His gaze drifted toward his cousin. "I coulda been a father, man," he said, his voice a mixture of awe and pain.

"Like our mothers always say, 'everything happens for a reason.'"

He dragged in a breath. "Yeah, whatever that reason may be."

Sterling gently clapped him on the shoulder. "In the meantime, we got a major project in the works, one that is going to make a big difference in the community. I'm living my best life, and you have two women to fill in any gaps that you choose."

Montgomery sputtered a laugh. "You are so right my brother." He lifted his glass. "To living our best life— for whatever the reason may be." As the soothing liquid moved down his throat he wondered if he could make Lexington part of the best life—even for a little while.

Lexington hung up the phone with Danielle Bovant, her assistant in Paris. They were slowly getting the hang of the six-hour time difference. She was happy to hear that the rehab project on a wing of the Musée du Quai Branly was well underway with no glitches so far. When they'd landed that deal she was beyond thrilled. This museum touched a special place in her. It was one of the few museums in Paris that embraced cultures beyond its own. It sat on the banks of the Seine, and was

touted for its non-European art and culture. Throughout the space there were rooms that paid homage to art
from Africa, Oceania, Asia and the Americas, as well as
contemporary Indigenous art. Sometimes she still had
to pinch herself when she thought about the shape she
was in when she'd left DC, and set up shop in France,
to where she was now. Randall Architect and Design
had developed a stellar reputation for excellence, orig-
inality and staying on budget. She always knew that
she had the skill and the vision to innovate and create
one-of-a-kind designs, but it wasn't until she'd put her
name on the door of her office that she fully understood
that she had more than what it took, even without her
father's blessing.

She checked the time on her cell phone: 3:30, then
adjusted the banker's lamp over her drafting table and
closely examined the measurements and confirmed
that each element would translate to scale. Satisfied
with the ground floor she flipped the page to the next
floor and continued her minute review until she was
satisfied, making minor adjustments when needed. She
was scheduled to meet with the engineer in the morning at Essex House to review the sketches and get the
blueprints underway. Everything needed to be perfect. Once the designs were fully approved, she could
begin using design software to turn the flat sketches
into three-dimensional representations, that could be
"toured" on a computer screen.

She switched off the lamp. That would mean seeing
Montgomery again. It would be the first time they were
together after the other night. She'd wanted to call him,
just to hear his voice, maybe invite him out for a drink,

or come up with some reason why they should talk about the project. Keep it casual. But decided against it every time the idea popped into her head. When she'd driven away from his home she wasn't certain just how far he wanted to take things. *No*, he wasn't seeing anyone, but he didn't indicate that he wanted to fill the blank spot with her. Obviously, it was only a good time between consenting adults to him. *Fine.*

She pushed away from the desk and stood. A flood of warmth flowed through her as the image of them together filled her vision. She dragged in a slow, deep breath, ran her tongue along her bottom lip hoping to reclaim the taste of him just as her cell phone rang.

She picked up the phone from the desk. Her pulse quickened when she recognized the number. "Hello."

"Hi. It's Monty."

Her heart thumped in her throat. "Hi. How are you? Everything okay? I signed the contract electronically. I hope that was okay."

"Oh, sure. Absolutely. That's pretty much how we do things these days." He cleared his throat. "I was wondering if you're not busy if we could meet?"

"Meet?"

"I have your deposit check. I thought maybe we could have an early dinner, drinks, drive, celebrate, seal the deal…see where the evening takes us."

She sucked on her bottom lip to keep from screaming and squeezed her eyes shut. "Um…sure. Did you have a time in mind?"

"I have some work to finish up here at the office. I can pick you up at seven."

If he picked her up then she would be at his mercy

for transportation. She shrugged with a smile. There was always Uber.

"Okay. Seven sounds good. I have some things to do here as well. I'm finishing up the sketches to review with the engineer tomorrow."

"Um, why don't you bring them with you…and pack an overnight bag. No telling how long the evening will last."

Her breath caught in her chest. "I can do that."

"Great. So, I'll see you at seven. Text me your address. Since we never made it there the other night."

"I will. See you at seven." She pressed the icon to end the call. A slow grin of pure delight spread across her face. Now to find the perfect outer and *under* outfit. In the meantime she needed to have a quick chat with her dad and bring him up to speed on the project—not that it would make a difference one way or the other. But she owed it to him. The business still carried his name.

She found her dad in front of the television watching a baseball game.

"Hey, Dad." She took a seat opposite him.

"Good game," he replied without tearing his eyes away from the screen.

"I wanted to talk to you about the business."

"Mmm-hmm."

"I'm going to pick up the deposit check for the job. I intend to open a new account with the money and transfer what is necessary to get the business out of the red. I'm also going to need your list of outside contractors to see if there is anyone I want to use."

He pursed his lips and finally looked at his daughter. "You seem to have it all figured out. I knew you would." He offered a half smile. "Should probably talk to your brother about the contractors."

Lexington rolled her eyes in frustration and pushed up from the seat. "Fine." She walked out unwilling to engage in a no-win battle with her father, as it was clear that he had already checked out. *Retired.* She would do everything in her power to save the family business. At least then she could return to Paris without a guilty conscience. What would happen to the business when she left? She'd figure it out. Like she always did.

She returned upstairs to get ready.

Just as she was checking her lipstick the front doorbell rang. Her heart bumped in her chest. She pulled in a breath, took a last look at her reflection, satisfied with the black sleeveless sheath that glided across her body in all the right places. She grabbed her purse and small overnight bag and went downstairs. When she got there Montgomery was being greeted by her father.

"I've heard a lot about you and the work you've been doing in DC," Lexington Sr. was saying.

"Trying to do my part, sir."

He clapped Montgomery on the back. "Real pleased that you picked my company to do this big job."

"Well, your daughter is very convincing." He threw her an appreciative look. "Her proposal stood head and shoulders above the rest."

"Yes, Lexi certainly has a way about her."

"Ready?" she interrupted.

"Sure." He extended his hand. "Good to meet you, Mr. Randall. Looking forward to this partnership."

"Good night, Dad." She walked past Montgomery and out onto the front steps. Montgomery followed.

"Everything okay?" He took her overnight bag.

"Fine," she murmured.

"I learned a long time ago that when a woman says 'fine,' it's far from it."

She slid him a sidelong glance. "Is that right?"

He smiled and opened the car door for her. "Yep." He moved closer. She could feel the warmth of his breath on her neck. "You look stunning by the way," he said, "And that dangerous dip in the back of this dress should have a warning sign."

She gave herself a moment to bathe in his nearness and the compliment. "Thank you," she murmured, got in and settled then angled her body toward Montgomery once he was behind the wheel. "You are right."

"About? The dress?" He winked, put the car in gear and pulled out.

"No. Issues with my dad. I'm trying not to let him make me crazy but it's not easy."

"The business, I take it."

He didn't need to know just how much trouble the business was in, so she skirted around the real problem. "Somewhat. I mean we're doing well," she lied. "It's just the whole disconnected position that my father has taken, and my brother..." She sucked her teeth in annoyance. "I won't even get into the level of pissed off I am with my brother."

Montgomery hummed deep in his throat. "You ever think that maybe what your father is doing is finally what he should have done a long time ago—turn the company over to you?"

She sighed. He *was* right, but not in the way that Montgomery imagined.

"So, uh what if that is the case, would you consider staying here?"

She eased back and turned to face the windshield. She wanted the question to mean more than she was sure it actually did. But he was only asking out of curiosity. Nothing more.

"That's not in my plans. I have my own business to run in Paris, remember?" She knitted her fingers together on her lap.

He didn't respond. Instead he leaned toward the console and pressed the icon for the sound system. "I put together a bunch of music that I like for driving. Hate to be at the mercy of a radio DJ." He tossed her a quick look as Jill Scott's "Whenever You're Around," pulsed through the speakers.

Lexington's head automatically started rocking to the smooth delivery and sultry rhythm. "Totally love Jill Scott," she said with her eyes half-closed.

Montgomery grinned. "I'm a card-carrying fan."

She turned her body toward him. "*Now* we can be real friends."

"I got plenty more where that came from. Who else besides Jill?"

"Hmm, I guess I'm kinda old-school for the most part. I'm a Motown girl at my core. Everything that came out of Motown is classic."

"We can definitely do old-school." He pressed a button on the dial as Jill's song ended and Marvin Gaye's "Distant Lover," live, filled the air around them.

"Oh, yes!" She slapped her thigh and hollered along

with the screaming crowd, which cracked Montgomery up.

"Marvin fan I take it," he said over his laughter.

She scrunched up her face in mild embarrassment. "Ya think?" She giggled. "I needed this," she said softly and rested her head back.

He gave her a quick look. "Night is still young. I'll make it be whatever you need it to be." He reached for her hand and brought it to his lips. "I promise you that."

The tingle from his lips slid up her arm. The air hitched for an instant in her chest. *Promises are made to be broken.* That was Michelle's favorite line. Inwardly she scoffed, but unfortunately it was true. The days of blindly believing in promises made by anyone other than herself were behind her. "Where are we going by the way?"

"Well, there's a new room opening tonight at the National Museum of African American History and Culture featuring ancient African architecture. I'd RSVP'd weeks ago and it totally slipped my mind until I got the alert on my phone. I apologize. But I thought it would be cool to check out and then dinner. *If* you want to," he finished with a lift of his brows.

"So... I'd be your plus-one?" she teased.

"Yes. My guest."

"You, uh hadn't planned on taking anyone," she hedged.

"Actually, no. Odd as it may seem I do a lot of these things alone or not at all."

Lexington studied his profile, which had settled into a thoughtful countenance, and something inside her shifted. In that brief instance she witnessed the tiny opening of a window to the true nature of Montgomery. For all of his oozing sexiness, career success, recognition in his field and the community—a man who could have any woman he wanted—he was nowhere near the playboy or ladies' man that the articles about him alluded to. *Don't let your mind go there.* Once this job was over it was back to Paris. *There's no room for wishful thinking. Just enjoy the moments.*

"I'd be happy to be your guest, Mr. Grant."

"Perfect!" His face lit up.

"The news of the museum's opening reached all the way to Paris. I've been dying to see it. I know the YouTube videos and Instagram posts don't do it justice."

He chuckled. "You're right about that. I've been at least a half-dozen times and I always find something that I missed."

But now you're going with me. That was at least a little special.

"You were definitely right," Lexington said as they slowly exited the museum two hours later. "It is absolutely incredible. I could spend weeks in there going over every inch. Our history is just so… I don't even have the words," she breathed, the awe-inspiring experience leaving her reflective.

Montgomery took her hand. "Which is why what we do, how we do it and who we do it for is so vital," he said, the passion of his convictions evident in his tone.

She looked at him as they crossed the plaza to the reserved parking lot. "So, when you buy a property or get buildings rehabbed or you do rentals or sales, that's the mission that you operate under?"

He nodded and pulled his key fob out of his pocket. The alarm chirped.

"Every time. One of the legacies of wealth is land and property ownership. For the most part black folks were stripped of those opportunities for wealth. As a result, there is an almost insurmountable gap that keeps us as an entire people playing behind the eight ball. Then as soon as we begin to establish foundational communities, here come the gentrifiers—modern day colonizers." He opened the door for her. "I plan to do everything I can to put planks on that bridge for as many of us to cross over as possible."

She turned to look into his eyes. *Damn it was too easy to fall for him. Now she had to add altruism and purpose to his list of attributes.* She leaned in and kissed him then slid into her seat without a word.

After a great meal that was punctuated with live entertainment at Bottomline, laughter, introspection, debates on who was the best Motown group, and their shared vision about Essex House, Montgomery drove them to his home.

"Can I get you anything?"

"Glass of wine would be nice."

"Coming up. Make yourself comfortable."

"Said the spider to the fly."

"Touché."

While he fixed her drink, she took out the rolled sketches from her overnight bag and spread them on the coffee table.

Montgomery took a seat next to her on the couch and handed her the glass of wine.

"Thank you."

"So…" He leaned forward. "Tell me all about it."

"Well…" She began with the sketches of the main floor and lobby that would provide conversational seating, a concierge station and mailroom. Beyond the main entrance was the small restaurant to the right and the gym to the left. Down the hallway were the business office, and two conference rooms and at the end of the corridor was the main ballroom. "I'll be hiring two assistants in the next few days to begin working with the vendors to select furnishings, paint colors, window dressing…"

"You'll supervise it all, right?"

"Absolutely. Nothing gets done without my approval. I don't want you to think I'm one of those obsessive micromanagers," she quickly added, "but anything that has my name attached has to be correct."

"I wouldn't expect anything less."

He studied her face for so long that she felt the flush rush from her throat to her cheeks. She blinked rapidly and he slid his gaze away.

Montgomery tilted his glass to his lips. "Show me more," he said, and she would have sworn that he in no way meant building sketches.

She cleared her throat and flipped to the next page that laid out the floor plans for the apartments. He'd moved closer, draped his arm along the back of the couch and turned his body in her direction making it almost impossible for her to concentrate.

And then his lips were brushing across the column of her neck. She sucked in a breath.

"I thought we were reviewing the sketches."

He teased away a tendril of hair with the tip of his finger and kissed that spot again. Her whole body went on high alert.

"I'm multitasking," he said and brought his mouth around to cover hers in a hot, wet kiss that at first only played with her lips until his tongue, sweetened by the bourbon dipped into her mouth.

She heard her own sigh mixed with his ragged groan and found herself being eased onto her back. His hands slid up her dress, caressed the inside of her thighs until she thought she would faint from the pleasure.

Her dress was up around her waist now, her black lace Victoria's Secret panties were on full display had either of them cared to look. His nimble fingers found the thin band of elastic that hugged her hips and pulled the flimsy material down to her knees. Before she could even think straight she gasped when his finger slid up inside her. She dug her fingertips into his shoulders, as her body with a will of its own rocked against his hand.

"Take this off," he urged between demanding kisses.

He raised up and she wiggled to a half upright position and tugged her dress over her head.

"Damn," he groaned, witnessing the perfect swell of her in front of him. He didn't even bother to unhook her bra, but simply pulled the straps and the cups down lifting her breasts even higher. He sucked a turgid nipple between his lips.

"Ohhh."

His hand slipped back down between her legs and he used two fingers this time, curving them within her. Her hips lurched upward. She nearly came. He'd touched that spot and she knew if he did it again it would be over for her. She felt her own wetness sliding over his fingers.

Somehow she managed to reach between them and tried to unfasten his belt and zipper. He moved her hands aside and did the honor.

She kicked away her panties until they hung on by only one ankle. He freed himself and seeing him again literally took her breath away. She maneuvered beneath him, draped one leg over the back of the couch and the other around his back.

When he pushed deep into her in the first single thrust, she saw heaven.

He'd promised himself that he wasn't gonna let great, hot sex turn him out, but every time he stroked inside her and she lifted up to meet him, moaned his name and turned her body over to him, whatever the hell promise he'd made to himself went out the window. He wanted her. All of her. Mind and body. He wanted to reach her soul and make it his. Crazy. He knew it was crazy, but that's how she made him feel when she kissed his ear, cried "*yes, yes, yes*," pressed her fingers into his back and made her insides suckle him like a newborn. She did that three-sixty thing again with her hips, and then her leg was up around his shoulder and he felt himself sink into the hot, wet, depths of her. He slid his hands beneath her, cupped her rotating behind tight, sealing them together until he felt the beauty of her orgasm shudder through her, and vibrate right through him. He let out a groan from the depths of his soul as he pulled out at the moment of release, bathing her belly in his essence.

The coming was so powerful that it literally left them giddy with laughter. They kissed and laughed and laughed and kissed some more.

Montgomery lifted his head to look in her eyes.

"You are amazing," he said softly.

She smiled and stroked his cheek.

Reluctantly he eased off and sat on the side of the couch next to her. "Don't move. I'll be right back." He stood, finding his legs a bit wobbly.

Moments later he returned with a small basin of sudsy water and a cloth, and with a tenderness that clenched her throat and brought tears to her eyes, he washed her breasts, her belly, her thighs, between her legs until she purred like a kitten.

No one had ever done that for her before and it left her feeling fragile, vulnerable, yet totally cared for as if with this tiny ritual he would protect her from all harm. But the thoughts frightened her back to the realization that this would not last. It couldn't. That's what she had to remember.

The following morning after an amazing breakfast and another stunning round of lovemaking they prepared for the day ahead.

"I don't see why we can't drive over together," Montgomery was saying as he stood in front of the bathroom mirror finishing up his morning shave.

"I won't give anyone the wrong idea. I need them all to know that I'm qualified for the job and not because I'm sleeping with the boss."

"I wouldn't call what we've been doing sleeping," he said with a chuckle.

She made a face at him in the mirror. "Very funny. But I'm serious." She sat on the end of the bed in her underwear and crossed her legs at the knee.

Montgomery turned. "Yeah, I get it. I do. So, I'll drive you home and you meet me over there? I have some things to take care of this morning anyway. So maybe around two?"

She bobbed her head in agreement.

He crossed the room and stood in front of her. She lifted her head to look up at him.

"I don't want you to think that what's happening between us is just a two-consenting-adult thing," he said. His dark eyes cinched and moved slowly across her face, as if searching for something behind what she hoped was a neutral expression, one that belied her racing pulse.

She teased her bottom lip with her tongue. "Then what is it?" she tossed back, in more of a challenge than a question.

He tucked his forefinger under her dimpled chin. "That's what I want us to take our time and find out."

Montgomery didn't wait for a reply. He bent down, kissed her lightly on the lips then walked away to finish dressing.

Lexington released the breath she'd held. Montgomery Grant was making this very difficult.

He'd opted to drive his black Suburban. It had the room he needed for the pit stops he had to make throughout the day, one of which was the supermarket. He wanted to stock up, seeing as that it appeared he and Lexi were going to be spending more nights and mornings together. His first stop, however, was to check on his B and B in Arlington and drop off some supplies. It was run by Greg and Melissa Williams, a married couple that had been together for thirty years. In their early seventies, spry, full of energy and ideas, running the first of his three B and B properties was their retirement dream come true. They managed the staff of five—a housekeeper, two chefs, a masseuse and a groundskeeper—as well as attended to the needs of the guests—in lieu of paying rent. The house pretty much ran itself, so the couple had plenty of time to relax on the veranda, tend to the small vegetable garden they'd cultivated, and look after their twin granddaughters who came to visit often. He'd have to remember to get a couple of Melissa's tomatoes to take home.

He pulled into the winding driveway of the three-story, six-bedroom house with the wraparound porch and ornate columns that guarded the front door. For some reason Greg believed he did a better job than the gardener in keeping the lawn and the hedges trimmed. So of course he was riding the lawnmower when Montgomery pulled up.

Greg cut the engine and cupped his hand over his eyes as Montgomery approached.

"Mr. Grant. Wasn't expecting you today." He climbed down off the machine and walked toward Montgomery. Greg Williams might be in his early seventies but he maintained the physique of a man half his age: broad shoulders and finely toned muscular arms and a hard six-pack that Montgomery could admire. The only give-away to his age was the full, gray with flecks of pepper, beard but it only seemed to add to his virile appearance. He wiped his hands on his well-worn jeans and extended his hand to Montgomery.

"How you doing, Mr. Williams?"

"All things considered I'm doing well." He chuckled. "What brings you out here today?"

The front door opened and Melissa stepped out onto the porch, dressed in a peach and white sundress that had her looking more like an ingenue than a grandmother. Melissa always reminded him of Lena Horne. She waved. "Just in time for brunch," she called out, and planted her hand on her hip.

The two men walked together to where Melissa stood.

"Mrs. Williams, as radiant as ever," Montgomery said with a big smile.

"I'll take that and any more that you have," she returned, with a squeeze to his shoulder. "Y'all come on in. I just finished making a shrimp salad. What brings you by?"

"I wanted to drop off the cases of water and a case of wine that my brother shipped to me. But…" They stepped into the wide foyer. "I wanted to speak with both of you about a proposition."

Laughter from one of the upper rooms drifted down to them.

Greg slowly closed the front door. Melissa turned, her head of auburn curls tipped to the side in question.

"Something wrong?" Melissa asked.

"No. No." He waved off their concerns. "Not at all."

"In that case," Melissa's full smile returned, "come on, let's sit and talk."

* * *

With a small bowl of Melissa's homemade shrimp salad and frosty glasses of iced tea in front of them, Montgomery broached his proposal. He'd been thinking about it for a while and although he hadn't run all the numbers, even Sterling agreed that it was the right thing to do and was in line with their mission of creating generational wealth.

Montgomery linked his fingers together and looked from one to the other. "You two have been amazing in running the B and B for the past three years. I could not have asked for better caretakers." He leaned in. "But I've given it a great deal of thought. I want to turn the place over to you fully paid for so that you in turn will have a piece of valuable property and land to pass on to your granddaughters."

Melissa's hand flew to her chest. Greg's mouth opened but he didn't utter a word. They both stared at him in disbelief.

"I know it sounds like a lot, but you both deserve it and I know you'll continue to nurture the property until you're ready to turn it over. The only thing I ask is that it stays in the family."

Tears slipped down Melissa's cheeks. Greg gripped her hand.

"I don't know what to say," Greg finally managed.

"Thank you," Melissa said for the both of them. "This is so overwhelming."

"I'll have the papers drawn up. You can review them with your family and we'll take it from there."

"So does this mean that after you turn the property

over to us, we won't see you anymore?" Melissa asked, her voice cracking.

"Not a chance!" He pushed to his feet. "As a matter of fact, there's someone I'd like you to meet. I might need to reserve a room one of these weekends."

"Ohhh," Melissa's brows rose. "You've never brought a young lady here before. She must be special."

Montgomery slowly nodded his head. "Yeah, she is." He wasn't sure if it would make a difference as to her decision to stay or go back to Europe. But he needed her to see another side of him and his vision. For whatever reason, what she thought about him and his world was important.

After Greg helped him unload the cases, he drove back into DC, arriving at Essex House a bit after one. That gave him some time to take a quick look around before Lexi arrived.

The crew was in the full throes of demolition. Now that the debris had been removed from all of the floors and rooms, they were stripping the building down to the studs, exposing wiring, plumbing and structural integrity. The spaces were even larger than he'd assessed. He could clearly see everything transformed under Lexington's creative vision. And from the looks of things, Gabriel had followed his instructions and brought on the extra crew members. There seemed to be a man in every corner of the building.

"Hey, Mr. Grant," Hank greeted as he walked over to where Montgomery stood in the center of the lobby floor. "Making good progress."

The two men shook hands.

"So I see," he agreed in admiration. "You're running a smooth sailing ship, Hank." He clapped the big man on the back.

"'Preciate that. Gabe got the extra crew and I gotta tell you, they are the hardest working men I've dealt with in a while. No job is too big or small."

Montgomery pursed his lips and slowly nodded in approval. "Really glad to hear it, Hank. I'm a big believer in second chances, especially for *us*."

"These men are going to be loyal to you for as long as you need them, just because you believe in them."

"As long as they do a good job, that's all I care about. Listen, I'm going to take a quick look around. I'm expecting a Ms. Randall in about a half hour. Her company got the architectural bid."

"Is that the one that you, uh, gave the tour to?" He gave up a half grin.

The earlier conversation he'd had with Lexi about precisely this jumped to the forefront of his thoughts.

Montgomery schooled his expression and threw an extra layer of seriousness in his tone. "Yes, she is. After my team reviewed all of the bids and the costs, Randall came out on top in every category. And the business is family and black owned. They are a staple in DC." Had he gone on too long? Protested too much?

"I am totally down with whomever you choose. This isn't our first rodeo together. I know that the projects you take on are always top-notch."

"We have done this a few times," he said with a chuckle. Hank had been with him from the beginning, his very first building rehab. "Anyway, I'm gonna take a look around. When Ms. Randall arrives I want to introduce her so they'll know who they're getting instructions from when we start putting this all back together."

"Will do. Here," he handed Montgomery a hard hat, "take this."

"Thanks." He put the hat on his head and walked toward a patch of men tearing down sheetrock.

Lexington was still in a foul mood after talking with her brother. He'd spent most of the hour-long phone conversation searching for a folder on his computer containing the names of previously employed subcontractors and vendors.

"I'll keep looking on this end, sis, but Dad is pure old-school. I'm sure he has the list in some folder somewhere."

"That's your answer, Max! Dammit. How did you let things get this bad? I mean I get it that your heart wasn't in it, but that's no reason for you to let things come to this." She dragged in an infuriated breath. "I want you to put everything that you have on your computer on a thumb drive and drop it off here tomorrow. Whatever loose invoices you have, bank statements, I want them. All of them. Tomorrow."

"Uh, tomorrow morning. Hmm, I can get them to you tomorrow night."

She squeezed her eyes shut. "Tomorrow night," she said wearily. "Now that we have the contract I have to hold up my end. The money will get us solvent again but not if I can't do my damned job!" The check with all those zeros that Montgomery had given her when he'd dropped her off that morning still had her blood pumping. Half now, the other half when she began buying the furnishings and appliances. This would put a dent in some of the business's outstanding bills, and put a stay on the move toward bankruptcy. If she could demonstrate to the court and their creditors that they could pay their debts she could save the company. One of the creditors had already threatened to put a lien on the house! The house that she grew up in. How did they let things get this bad? She could pull it off. She knew she could. The main thing was never to let Montgomery know that he'd gotten into bed "literally" with a company that was being held together by hope and bubble gum, and that his investment was actually going to bail out Randall Architect and Design.

"Don't F this up, Max."

"All right. All right. I'll have the information tomorrow night."

She'd sighed, but was mildly appeased because she'd used the house landline and she could slam the phone in Maxwell's ear.

It had started to drizzle just as she pulled up in front of Essex House. The entire building was draped in the skeleton of scaffolding and metal mesh. Even with the windows closed she could hear the thrilling sound of men at work, hammering and ripping and nailing and tossing… She exhaled, gathered her things and got out of the car. Hopefully she wouldn't run into Gabriel, especially after the morning she'd had with her brother.

She darted across the street and beneath the protection of the scaffolding as the drizzle began to pick up steam.

The front entrance was now blocked by the green wood walls that had gone up around the periphery of the building. Warning notices declaring it was a hard hat area and that construction was underway, along with a host of permits, were plastered strategically on the green planks. The makeshift door had a square Plexiglas window. She peeked inside. From what she could see a lot had been accomplished since the last time she was there. She reached for the circular hole in the wood that stood in for a doorknob.

"I thought that was you. I'd know those legs anywhere."

For a moment she squeezed her eyes shut and gritted her teeth, willing herself to tap down her annoyance. She turned around slowly, hoping that her expression was neutral.

"Hello, Gabriel." Her stomach knotted.

He drew closer and leaned in to kiss her cheek. She smoothly stepped aside. Gabe snorted a laugh.

"It's like that, huh?"

"Like what, Gabe? Like there is no 'that.' There is nothing. Okay?" She adjusted her oversize leather tote on her shoulder.

He held up his hands. "Hey, relax." He paused a beat, frowned. "What are you doing back here, or am I not allowed to ask?"

"I'm the architect for this project." She folded her arms.

The rain was coming down hard now, slapping against the makeshift roofing, bouncing of the street.

The corner of one side of his mouth curved upward. "So you got it. Guess congratulations are in order. Used that Randall charm, huh?"

Pure willpower kept her from smacking the smug look off his face and the words back down his throat.

"Screw you, Gabe," she snapped, pointing a finger at his chest. "I don't need to use charm and BS to get through life. I actually have skill and experience and an MIT education to back it up." Fury whipped through her. Her nostrils flared as she sucked in air.

"Hey," he held up his hands in submission. "That was out of line. I'm sorry." He paused then repeated his apology.

She took a step back, dragged in a calming breath.

"Listen, since it looks like we're going to actually be working together on some level or the other, can we try to get along. Pretend?"

She cut her eyes at him. "Whatever, Gabriel."

"That's a start. Let's get out of this weather." He reached around her and pulled the heavy door open. "After you."

On her drive over, Montgomery texted to tell her to check in with his foreman Hank Forbes when she arrived. *The big guy*, he'd added to fuel her memory. She'd smiled. Hank Forbes was a hard man to forget. The one thing she did remember was that for all of his height and girth he had the kindest eyes and most soothing demeanor of anyone she'd ever met.

Once inside the noise intensified, as raised voices competed with the sounds of banging and drilling.

"I need to find Hank," she shouted to Gabriel over the din.

There was a table at the entrance lined with hard hats. Gabriel grabbed one and gave it to Lexington. "You'll need this."

She rolled her eyes, and pulled out the hard hat she had in her supply bag.

"I shoulda known." He put the extra hat back on the table and put on the hard hat that he'd had hooked to his belt. "Hank is probably down this hallway."

Lexington reluctantly followed him, hating that she was relying on him for anything.

"He's right over there," Gabriel said, pointing out Hank. "Watch your step. Okay."

When she looked at him, actually looked at him, for an instant the Gabriel Martin that she'd known and fallen in love with appeared in the softness of his eyes, the curve of his smile. Then just as quickly the image and the sensation was gone, replaced by the memory of what he'd done.

"Thanks."

He turned and walked away. Lexington headed in the direction of Hank, who was supervising two workers that were pulling down a wall.

"Watch the support beams," Hank shouted. He wiped his forehead and turned just as Lexington approached. His face lit up. "Ms. Randall. I would take off my hat." He chuckled and she noticed again the perfect smile and even white teeth.

She felt that knot in her stomach slowly unwind. "I totally get it. I'm supposed to meet Mont… Mr. Grant," she said, catching herself.

"Yeah, he told me. I'll radio him, let him know you're here."

"Thank you."

Hank used the walkie-talkie and moments later she heard Montgomery's voice crackling in the air. Just the sound of his voice got her all hot and flushed. In the midst of all the dust and noise and rubble, the image of them together, the way he touched her, made her feel, blocked all that other stuff out.

"He'll be down in a few," Hank was saying, snapping Lexington back to the moment.

She blinked. "Great."

"I can take you over to our makeshift office. A little more comfortable."

"'Preciate that."

Lexington sat down on the hard wood chair, dug in her bag and took out her cell to check for messages.

"You are a welcome sight."

She glanced up to see Montgomery leaning in the doorway.

"I would walk over and kiss that sexy mouth of yours, but I don't want folks to talk." He winked.

She slowly rose to her feet. "Maybe if you're nice I'll let you make it up to me later."

His brows rose. "I plan to hold you to that, *Ms.* Randall." He tipped his head toward the bustling main floor. "Come on. Let me formally introduce you to everyone."

Montgomery introduced her to the workers as teams. There was the team that dealt with the disposal of material, others that took down the walls, others that checked pipes and others that put up temporary framing. Hank was responsible for the supervision of the teams, but it was Gabriel who was the project manager and dealt with the smooth flow and oversight of the entire operation. He was the one that approved the progress, step by step, and reported to Montgomery. She would definitely try to limit their interactions to the bare minimum. The next few months were going to test her patience and the vow that she'd made with herself to keep Gabriel Martin in her rearview.

Six

It would still be a few weeks before Lexi would be able to get in and begin doing her thing with the spaces. In the meantime she got together with the engineer who reviewed her sketches and they worked to prepare the final blueprints that were approved by Montgomery, Hank and Gabriel.

Of course, Maxwell didn't come through as promised, so Lexington had to scour through her father's old receipts and notes to locate a few possible candidates to help out once she was able to begin her portion of the work. At some point she was going to have to dive into the accounting records with a fine-tooth comb, especially before depositing any money into the business account.

Her one looming worry was that Montgomery would

discover that the company was more of a front than a reality.

Keeping secrets wasn't something that she was comfortable with, knowing all too well how secrets could ruin everything in their path, but now she didn't know how to go backward and undo the facade she'd put up. She opened her desk drawer and looked at the envelope that contained the deposit check and took it out. She'd deposit it into her account and make incremental transfers to the business account to begin clearing some of the debt. But until she took a hard look at the ledgers there was no way that she would simply dump $100,000 into the account.

"Hey, bruh," Sterling greeted, appearing in Montgomery's office doorway.

He glanced up from the papers on his desk. "Hey, how's it going?"

Sterling strode in and took a seat, propped his ankle on his knee and leaned back. "Checking on you. I took care of the paperwork for the Williams family. You want me to send it to them directly or to their attorney?"

Montgomery stroked his chin. "Give them a call and see what they want to do."

Sterling nodded. "Not a problem." He paused a beat. "The real estate team lined up some properties for Stella to take a look at."

Montgomery's jaw tightened. He nodded his reply.

"You talk to her again?"

"No."

"We really haven't talked any more about…what she told you. You good?"

Montgomery leveled his cousin with a steady gaze. "If I was to say that what she told me about her illness and about…our child, didn't affect me, I'd be lying." He leaned back in his seat. "But there's nothing I can do about it except move on, which is exactly what I plan to do."

His intercom buzzed. He pressed the flashing button. "Yes, Cherise."

"Ms. Vincent is on the line for you."

He flashed Sterling a look. "I'm sure it's about an update on the housing search. Cherise, can you handle it?"

"No problem."

Montgomery pursed his lips but before he could say anything the intercom buzzed again.

"Yes?"

"She says she needs to speak with you and it's not about housing."

He blew out a breath. "Fine. I'll take it."

"She's on line two."

He gave Sterling a "you can go" look, which he ignored.

"You need a wingman," he mouthed.

Montgomery pressed the button flashing for his attention.

"Stella. What can I do for you?" He listened. A frown tightened the line between his brows. "Why?" He pushed a folder aside. "That's not why I'm doing this. If you know anything about me you should know that much." He picked up a pen and rubbed it between his fingers. "I'll think about it and get back to you. Yes. By the end of the week. Sure. Goodbye."

His hand seemed to move in slow motion as he returned the phone to the cradle.

Sterling's foot dropped to the floor. He leaned forward, resting his arms on his thighs. "Well, what was that about?"

Montgomery ran his hand across his face as if the action would somehow wash away the past few minutes.

"Obviously it's not about real estate," Sterling added.

"No. This new job of hers at the television station— she's one of the producers. She pitched a segment focusing on the gentrification of black communities. She wants to feature MG Holdings and Essex House in particular."

"Okay? And that's a bad thing how?"

Montgomery glanced away. "I'm just real hesitant to…have to deal with Stella on any level. Too many bad feelings, at least on my end."

"Understandable. But this is a good opportunity for us, the business and the work that we do here." He pushed to his feet. "You're a big boy, cuz. Think of the broader picture. Besides, you've moved on—apparently with our lady architect."

He lifted his chin in agreement. "True." He folded his hands on top of his desk. "And I want to give that relationship my full attention—for as long as it lasts."

"Then go for it. Stella is past tense. She's doing her job, probably wants to show her bosses what she's got, and you'll do yours. It's only going to go beyond that if you let it."

Montgomery puffed his cheeks then blew out air. "You're right. I'm not in this for the recognition, but shining a spotlight on what we do might encourage others to do the same thing."

"Exactly. Take the opportunity and make it yours. End of story. No pun intended."

Montgomery tipped his head to the side, suddenly inspired. "As a matter of fact, I think we need to do this together. Me and you."

"What? Naw. This is your lane."

"And it needs to be yours, as well. You're the engine that keeps things running. I'm the vision. Can't have one without the other."

Sterling pushed to his feet and adjusted his gleaming white shirt at the waist. "I'll think about it and get back to you."

"Nothing to think about, bruh. We do this together." He extended his hand toward his cousin.

Sterling shook his head, chuckling as he clasped Montgomery's hand. "They don't call you the 'deal maker whisperer' for nothing," he teased. "You think the DC audience is ready for the both of us at once?" he asked, stroking his low-cut tapered beard.

"I'm sure they'll manage. I'll have Cherise give Stella a call and get everything set up."

"Cool." He turned to leave. "Told you that you needed a wingman." He winked and walked out.

Montgomery spun his high-backed leather seat toward the window that faced downtown DC. The spire of the Washington Monument cut into the waning afternoon sky. Sterling was right about the wingman part. He didn't have a good feeling about this for a variety of reasons, mainly the bad taste he still had in his mouth about what Stella had done, or rather *how* she had done it. While he empathized with her reasons, he still could not get past the fact that after all that he thought they meant to each other she didn't trust him enough to tell him the truth. That she would get rid of their child without telling him—for years. Yes! He understood that her health was on the line, but she should have told him. And if she was the kind of woman that would do that to someone that she claimed to love, what else might she do if she was backed into a corner or had to decide how she would come out on top no matter who might be hurt in the process? *That* was the woman he saw now. Not the Stella Vincent that he'd once wanted to marry. He might be totally wrong. But worst case scenario he could be right. And if so, he wanted his guard up.

After returning from the bank, Lexington carefully reviewed the résumés of ten potential assistants. She needed at least two. After reviewing their digital résumés, she'd pretty much settled on three. They were all relatively local, which was good. One had attended Cooper Union, the other two graduated from Pratt Institute and Virginia Polytechnic Institute, but best of all they were all black women. One of her goals as she carved out her career was that every chance she got to support a qualified black woman she was going to do it. She remembered all too well being the doubled-edged sword "only one": the only woman, and the only woman of color in her classes, in meetings, on jobs. She couldn't transform the entire industry, but she could make a difference; one woman, one project at a time.

She picked up her cell phone and checked the time. It was only ten thirty. Early. Hopefully, she could set up some interviews and get the process underway. Her first call was to Ashanti Dixon who readily agreed to meet at noon. The call to Laverne Mitchell went to voicemail. The third call she hit pay dirt again and scheduled a three o'clock with Nia Fields.

With that task out of the way, she hurried off to the kitchen to prepare some light snacks and make sure there was fresh coffee, and iced tea as an alternative. She printed out copies of their résumés and did a last look around the small office to make sure it was presentable and representative of a small, but successful family business. Then she placed a call to her brother.

She could hear music in the background when he answered. She rolled her eyes.

"Max."

"Hey, sis." The music lowered. "I was in the middle of setting up a session with a new girl group. They are crazy talented."

"That's wonderful," she said, gritting her teeth. "Listen, I've set up some interviews for this afternoon to hire two assistants for the Essex House project."

"Yeah," he said as if that was an odd comment to make. "That's cool. Glad to hear things are moving along."

"Do you want to be here?" She could almost see his handsome face crease in confused annoyance.

"Why, sis? The last person you need sitting on the sidelines is me. You handle it. Like I said when you got back, my head is not in the family business. Hasn't been for a while. I'm fine with you removing my name from company records." He cleared his throat. "Look, the business should have always been yours. I don't have a problem with that. I have to go. I have people coming."

She blew out a breath, a mixture of frustration and relief. "Have a good session." She disconnected the call before he could respond. "I tried," she groused. It was merely a courtesy that she called him in the first place. Truth be told she was glad he was out. The meeting would run much more smoothly without Maxwell Randall raining his damn-near irresistible charm all over the women.

Meanwhile, she wouldn't allow her brother to distract her from what she needed to do. She jogged up to her bedroom to change out of her errand-running jeans and T-shirt into a black sleeveless jersey dress that hit just above her knees. She added silver hoops to her ears and a single strand silver chain, so delicately thin that it could have been an illusion. Stepping into her black heels, she did a last check in the mirror, patted the perfectly shaped bun on top of her head, and added a coat of gloss to her lips just as the doorbell rang.

She closed the lipstick case, dropped it on top of her dresser and went down to meet her first interviewee.

She pulled the door open and came up short.

"Monty…" she said on a startled breath. A full-blown smile tugged at her mouth. "What are you doing here?"

His dark eyes dragged hungrily over her body then checked beyond her shoulder, and with the coast clear he pulled her flush against him and covered her mouth with his.

She leaned into the hard lines of his body as if being mildly ravaged in the doorway of her family home was an everyday occurrence. She cupped the back of his head, dove deeper into their kiss.

The sudden sound of a truck rumbling down the street tugged them back to reality.

Montgomery stepped back with his gaze locked on her face. He ran his tongue along his bottom lip. "Sweet," he murmured. His eyes sparked with seductive mischief.

Lexington tugged in a breath and slowly exhaled. She bit back a grin. "What are you doing here?"

He leaned casually against the door frame, his long sculpted body an object of desire, and what she really wanted to do was drag him up to her bedroom by his belt loops and make love with him until they passed out.

"All I've been thinking about is you and when we'd see each other again," he murmured low in his throat.

"You could have called," she said coyly.

"Humph, I don't think a phone call would have done the trick."

She ducked her head and laughed then looked him in the eyes, trying to be serious. "Well, believe it or not, I'm working."

He looked her up and down. "Dressed like that?"

She folded her arms. "As a matter of fact, yes. I'm interviewing for an assistant. There will be a ton of tasks to take care of and I go into every job fully prepared."

He nodded his head. "Makes sense." He frowned. "Uh, are you leaving to meet up or are they coming here?"

"Here." She looked around him at a woman with stunning dreadlocks twisted in an intricate pile on her head coming down the short lane to her front door. "This is her."

He glanced over his shoulder. "I better go. Got what I came for." He winked. He started to walk away.

"Hey. Wait. You might as well meet her. I think it'll be good for her to know who we're working for—*if* I decide to take her on."

He gave a light shrug. "If you're sure."

She nodded quickly, just as Ashanti crossed the first step on the porch. Monty stepped to the side.

"Ms. Dixon." Lexington extended her hand.

"Hello. Please call me Ashanti," she said, shaking Lexington's hand.

Lexington smiled. "Your timing is perfect. This is Mr. Grant. The owner of Essex House."

"Oh!" Her eyes widened. She shook his hand. "It's a pleasure to meet you. I've followed your work across DC. Impressive."

He chuckled. "She's hired."

They all laughed. "I'll call you," he said to Lexington. "Nice to meet you." He strode off.

"Please come in."

Lexington wasn't quite sure if she'd hired Ashanti because she had all the skills she needed for the project, or if she hired her simply because she couldn't concentrate after the impromptu visit by Montgomery.

"Thank you so much for the opportunity, Ms. Randall," Ashanti was saying after she'd reviewed the contract agreement and signed it.

Lexington blinked. "Looking forward to working with you. It will be a couple of weeks before we can actually dive in, but I want to start looking at a list of vendors. One day next week I'd like to bring you with me to tour the site. I'll email you the designs for review."

They walked to the front door.

"I can get started on compiling the vendor list."

"That's great. I'll get those to you by the end of the day."

"Thank you again," Ashanti said.

Lexington closed the door, turned and pressed her back against it. She wondered what Monty was doing right now. But she didn't have time to think about it at the moment, her next potential assistant was due any minute.

Montgomery returned to his office after leaving Lexington. But leaving her didn't lessen his desire for her. Seeing her in that black number that teased her curves only heightened his lust. It was crazy. She occupied all of the spaces in his head, making it hard to focus on anything other than feeling her beneath him. So, the last thing he wanted to think about was the session with Stella.

When he'd come back to the office there was a message on his desk that Stella would like to bring the camera crew to the site to get some location shots prior to their interview. He crumpled the message and tossed it in the trash. He walked out of his office and down the hall in search of his cousin.

Sterling was in the copy room.

"Hey, got a few minutes?"

Sterling looked up from the pages spitting out of the machine. "Sure. Whatsup?"

Montgomery slid his hands into the pockets of his slacks. "Got a message from Stella."

"Yeah." He gathered his copies.

"She wants to come by the site to get some footage."

"Problem?"

Montgomery sighed. "I don't know, man. I keep thinking that I shouldn't have agreed."

Sterling tilted his head. "Thought we got beyond that."

They walked together down the hallway toward Sterling's office. Sterling stopped in his doorway. "Hey, whatever you decide, I got your back. But I still think it's a good idea. Let me know what day she plans to come and I'll be sure to be there if that will help."

Montgomery nodded. "All right. Thanks, man." He clapped him on the shoulder and walked off.

When he got back to his office, Cherise handed him another message from Stella, asking to call her as soon as possible. Inwardly he groaned.

"She said she's going to take the apartment we found for her," Cherise said.

"Thanks." One thing out of the way. He opened his office door and shut it behind him. His cell phone buzzed in his pocket. He pulled it out and his mood immediately lifted.

"Hey, gorgeous."

Her musical laughter filled his soul.

"Hey, yourself." She paused a beat. "That was really… unexpected you turning up this afternoon."

"I should have called. I really apologize."

"No need. I liked it," she cooed.

His body warmed all over. "So did I. I haven't stopped thinking about you."

"I thought we could pick up where we left off."

"Ohhh. I like the sound of that. It's going to be a beautiful night. Pack a bag, come by my place and I'll put something edible on the grill."

She laughed. "Edible. Is that all you can say?"

"I've even gone grocery shopping, and I think I'll surprise you with my culinary skills, Ms. Randall."

She giggled again. "I'll hold you to it."

"Eight work for you?"

"See you then."

Montgomery checked the time on his phone. He had a solid three hours to get home and plan the perfect evening for the sexiest woman he ever knew. He started for the door and realized he still had Stella's message in his hand. He glanced at Cherise's neat handwriting.

He punched the numbers in on his cell while he walked out the door. Stella answered on the second ring.

"Oh, thanks for calling back."

"Sure. What's up, Stella?"

"Wellll, I was thinking that I could fix dinner for you…to thank you for finding me that fabulous apartment. I signed the lease this morning. Move in next week."

"Uh, that's great, Stella. Glad it worked out. But I have plans." He waved good-night to Cherise and went down the corridor. He pressed the button for the elevator.

"Oh. Business meeting?" she hedged.

His jaw flexed. "No."

She was quiet. "I'm sorry. It's none of my business.

Well, the offer still stands. Maybe you can stop by the new place once I get settled."

The elevator doors slid open and he stepped in. "I'm on the elevator. We'll probably get cut off. I'll have Cherise schedule a time for you to come to the site."

As he expected the call cut off, and none too soon.

Montgomery leaned down and kissed the back of Lexington's neck, inhaling the heady scent of her that drove him insane. "More wine?"

She lifted her head toward him and held up her glass. "Sure."

He gave her a refill.

"Food smells delicious."

He glanced at her over his shoulder as he turned the salmon. "Can you do me one small favor?"

"Anything…" she said in a comically wispy voice.

He chuckled. "Would you bring the salad from the fridge and whatever dressing you like."

"Sure." She pushed up from the lounge chair and went through the house to the kitchen.

When she returned several minutes later she found the wood table adorned with a white linen table cloth and two scented candles enclosed in glass bowls that flickered erotically in the night. He was putting two dinner plates on the table.

"You do this for all the girls?" she asked, coming up alongside him. She set down the salad and two bottles of dressing.

Montgomery slid his arms around her and pulled her close. "Only one girl. You." His eyes slow danced across her face before he slowly leaned in to kiss her.

Lexington sighed against his mouth and melded her body into his. His hands glided along her waist before cupping her tight. He groaned before slowly pulling away. "We should probably eat," he said, his voice ragged. He kissed her lips.

She sighed. "Yeah, that might be a good idea."

Her wicked smile teased him. He released her. "I'll fix your plate."

Full, relaxed under a canopy of a sprinkling of stars and a half-moon, with some old-school Smokey Robinson playing in the background, they sipped wine and talked in soft voices animated by laughter. Easy. Natural. As if this was always their thing. When Smokey's "Ooo Baby, Baby" finished, Luther's silky crooning filled the space with "If This World Were Mine."

Montgomery turned his head toward Lexington and gently lifted her glass from her fingers and set it on the circular table between them. He took her hand.

"I let you slide with Smokey, but not Luther."

"Monty," she giggled.

"Come on, woman, lemme see what you got." He helped her to her feet and she stepped into his embrace.

"Be careful what you wish for," she whispered before resting her head on his shoulder.

"…I would place at your feet," Montgomery crooned in soft harmony.

"If this world were miiiiinee," Lexington sang.

"Whoaaa oh…" they harmonized.

Lexington drew her head back and looked into Monty's eyes that seemed to sparkle in the night light. "We make a pretty good duet," she said, smiling at him.

Montgomery fingered the shell of her ear. "Yeah, we do."

Her heart thumped. His voice was low and full of meaning which she didn't dare try to decipher. Instead she gave into the demand of his kiss and the flames of lust she'd felt simmering between them since that afternoon.

When he made love to her, he was different this time, not in *how* he loved and awakened every part of her, but the *way* he loved her. Something had changed in him. His movements inside her were deeper somehow, slower, almost surreal as if he was on the cusp of discovery yet longed for the finding to last. His touch, always electrifying, seemed to now summon the very essence of her being to rise up to meet him on a plane she'd never traveled. She could feel the intensity of the pull, the complete yielding of her body to him. She was frightened by the power of the sensations that rose and fell and rose again from the soles of her feet to the top of her head. The room seemed to turn and the stars and half-moon glistened behind her closed lids. The tidal wave roared toward her and there was nothing she wanted to do but succumb to its power. She came on him so hard that her cry of release caught and hung in the air. Her held her through it, dove in and out of the wave, kissed away the tears and just when the last of her orgasm began to wane and her body's shuddering eased, he stroked that spot deep inside. She gasped for air. Her hips arched. He rose up on his knees, spread her legs wide, holding them apart as he stroked her in places that had never been reached, his head tossed back in the throes of his climax that exploded like Mount St. Helens between them.

Several moments passed with them clutching for air. With great reluctance and what remained of any energy, Montgomery rolled over onto his back. He threw his arm across his eyes and heaved in a breath.

Lexington could still feel her heart pound in her chest and the tiny sparks of electricity pop in her veins. What was that? What had just happened between them? The other times were mind and body altering, making her realize she hadn't experienced great sex until Monty. But this time was—she didn't know what it was. She imagined it was when the moment of loving someone was realized. That instant in time.

But that couldn't be it because it would ruin everything. She squeezed her eyes shut and silently repeated that mantra over and over until she almost believed it. But, when he turned on his side to face her, and with a tenderness that put a knot in her throat, he kissed her and whispered… *"Stay."*

Standing under the beat of the shower, Montgomery mentally chastised himself for what he'd said. *What were you thinking? Stay. Really, Monty. What the hell is wrong with you? You are getting too caught up in a woman who will be gone in six to eight months. Then what?*

Lathering his body he let the soapy water slide off him. He braced his palms along the shower wall, allowing the pulsing water to ride down his spine, a part of him wishing that he could wash away this all-encompassing feeling that he had for Lexington. Truth—he was beyond that now. The problem: What was he going to do about it?

When he walked out of the bathroom, the aroma of coffee beckoned him to the kitchen.

"Hey," he greeted, seeing her turn to him with a sexy-ass smile that made him feel off balance.

"Hmm, aren't you all fresh and brand new," she teased. "Hope you don't mind. I got the coffee going."

"Not at all." He walked over and kissed her lightly on the lips. "My space is yours." He swallowed. "For whenever and whatever," he quickly added. He filled his coffee mug. "So you're now running businesses on two continents, woman. How does that feel?" He plopped down on the counter stool and looked at her over the rim of his mug.

She grinned and pushed out a breath. "If I think about it that way it may seem daunting." Her expression sobered. "But I know what I want." She slid onto a stool beside him. "I have good people. I understand business and my goal is to be the best at what I do. Not second. *The* best."

"Well, I can't wait to see your vision come to life at Essex House. The sketches don't do it justice."

"Thanks. Me, too. I'm eager to get started. And now that I have my team—we're just waiting on y'all," she teased and tapped the tip of his nose with her finger. "Speaking of team and work I need to get home. I have a meeting at eleven with my two assistants, Ashanti and Nia, to start mapping out plans and responsibilities. Each of them has a different skill set, so I want to make sure that it's used to maximize their talents. Makes for a successful partnership and project."

He finished off his coffee. "You're absolutely right. That's why Sterling and I work so well together. The fact that we actually like each other certainly helps, but he brings things to the table that I don't and vice versa."

"And that is why Essex House is gonna be all that and then some." She gave him a quick kiss. "Gotta run. Call me later?"

"Will do."

He listened to the front door close and felt an empty space open up inside him, and knew he had to continue being with her to keep it filled. That was the easy part. Keeping a rein on his emotions was another.

During the day they fulfilled their obligations to their respective businesses. At night they fulfilled their obligations to each other, growing more close with each pairing.

Lexington thought about that now, how her life was nothing that she expected it to be when she'd returned from Europe. The last thing on her mind was getting into a relationship that had her questioning her plans for the future. Now, leaving here, leaving Montgomery was too hard to think about. So, she tried not to, immersing herself in her work, approving purchase orders that Ashanti had placed while Nia negotiated with suppliers, and scouring the company accounts. The more she tried to make sense of where things went wrong with Randall Architect and Design, the more concerned she became. Too much didn't make sense. Sure, business wasn't that great. They didn't have the level of projects they once did, but that did not account for the inexplicable holes in the finances. Money had clearly come in, and it went out, yet vendors and suppliers were either not paid on time, in full or at all. She didn't want to give voice to the dark thought running through her head. There had to be an explanation. Maybe it was simple math errors. Dad wasn't the greatest with the computer system although Max could hold his own. Maybe it was as simple as that.

She blew out a breath of exhaustion. She'd been staring at the screen for nearly two hours. Ashanti and Nia would be on their way to Essex House to meet her. She planned to give them a tour so they'd have more of a perspective on the scope of their work. Based on the timeline, the interior structure should be shored up. The electrical work was all but completed, and the drywall and plastering would be well underway.

She turned off the computer, promising herself to get back to that mess later. She grabbed her tote, car keys and phone and headed out.

By the time Lexington found a place to park, Ashanti and Nia were pulling up in Nia's black SUV, which always reminded her of the Secret Service vehicles that tried and failed to be incognito on the streets of DC.

Lexington got out and listened for the chirp of her car alarm. Satisfied, she waved them over as they emerged from the vehicle.

Ashanti and Nia were a perfect match. They complimented each other in skill and temperament. Ashanti had an amazing eye for the most minute detail in a color, like the way a single thread wove through fabric or how the most impossible combinations of form, texture and design could look seamless. Nia lived up to her name of *purpose*. She was purposeful in all that she did, never missing a detail, a number out of place, the timetable for deliveries and the organization of every receipt and purchase order. Nia was the more quiet of the two, pensive almost, where Ashanti had a comment or eye-opening observation on just about everything and everyone. But best of all they actually seemed to like each other. She couldn't have been happier with her decision.

"Hey, ladies. Thanks for meeting me here."

"I've so been looking forward to this," Ashanti said. "I hope we can see as many of the spaces as possible." Her gaze rose upward, taking in the structure.

"This was the only day and time that worked for our schedules," Nia noted. "Says 'construction zone,'" she observed pointing to the sign plastered on the scaffolding. "Don't we need hard hats?"

"Got them right here," Lexington assured her, popped open the trunk of her car and took out one for each of them.

Ashanti smirked in admiration. "Awesome."

Lexington winked. "Right this way, ladies."

As she pulled open the door she thought she probably should have given Monty a heads-up that she was bringing her assistants. They'd tossed it around in conversation, but never settled on a date. Inwardly she shrugged. He probably wasn't here anyway, and if he was, all the better. She'd get to see him in the middle of the day.

When she pulled open the door, surprise slowed her step. Not only had an incredible amount of work been done, but there was a film crew set up in what would eventually be the lobby.

"I'm ready for my close-up," Ashanti said over her

giggle. "What's going on? Are we going to be on television?"

"To tell you the truth I really don't know," she said slowly, as her gaze spanned the space and landed on Montgomery in a semi-lit corner talking very close to some woman. Her cheeks flushed. *Why does she keep touching his arm?*

"You okay, Lexi?" Nia asked.

She blinked and over a tight-lipped smile she nodded yes.

Hank lumbered over. "Ms. Randall. How are you?"

"Good. Thanks." Her brows knitted. "What's with the cameras?"

"Oh, local television station is gonna be doing a segment on the building." He lifted the hard hat from his head and wiped his forehead with a cloth from his back pocket. "Came today to take some shots of the work in progress. Ain't that what you're here for?" He set the hat back on his head.

"Uh, no. Actually I came to give my two new assistants a tour." She introduced Ashanti and Nia to Hank. "They may be stopping by from time to time."

"Fine with the boss, it's fine with me."

"Is that the person in charge?" she asked, lifting her chin in the direction of Montgomery and Stella.

Montgomery must have sensed her because at that precise moment he turned and looked in her direction. If she didn't know better she would have sworn that she saw something other than pleasure at seeing her in his expression.

"Yep. Works for the station," Hank was saying. "Well, I gotta get back to work."

"Sure. Thanks, Hank," she murmured, not taking her eyes off Montgomery.

"Where should we start?" Ashanti wanted to know. She'd unwound the intricate twists of her hair and let the locs drop down her back to make way for the hard hat.

"At the beginning," Lexington joked, hoping to lighten her mood with her tone. She started to lead them off, when Montgomery's voice caught her from behind. She schooled her expression and turned around.

"Hi. I didn't know you were stopping by today."

Did he look nervous, guilty or was she projecting? "I wanted Ashanti and Nia to have a look at the spaces. Helps in the decision process." She knew her tone was aloof but she couldn't help it.

"Mr. Montgomery. Good to see you again," Ashanti greeted taking some of the tension out of the air.

"Yes, good to see you as well."

"This is Nia Fields," Lexington managed. "She'll be working with me as well."

Montgomery shook her hand. "Pleasure."

"I'm sorry I didn't *know* that a camera crew would be here today," she said, being particularly catty and enjoying watching him shift his weight under the veiled accusation of her words.

But before he could respond, the woman he'd been cozied up with came over.

"Sorry to interrupt, Monty," she said, again putting her hand possessively on his arm, "but we need you up on the second floor. I want to get a few shots while we've got good light." She tossed Lexington a cursory glance and a tight-lipped smile.

He eased out of her grip on his arm. "Lexington Randall, this is Stella Vincent. She works at WJLA and is doing a segment on Essex House. Ms. Randall is the architect and interior designer for the project."

Stella's brow arched over greenish-brown eyes. She put on a megawatt smile, her jet-black pixie haircut outlining her oval face. "Impressive. You have quite the project on your hands."

"I'm looking forward to the challenge." She smiled, leveling her gaze at Stella.

"Indeed. Well," she hitched a breath. "Nice to meet you, Laura."

"Lexington."

She shook her head and pursed her melon-tinted lips. "Silly me. I am so sorry. Have a million things on my mind."

"Really?" Lexington quizzed as if the possibility was utterly impossible, and relished in the flash of Stella's eyes. "Have a good shoot." She turned to join her team. Ashanti had apparently been swept up in the charm of Sterling Grant, as they were off to the far side in close conversation. Nia was busy taking copious notes. And then she felt a hand on her arm.

She looked down at Montgomery's hand as if he was some beggar that dared to accost her. Her lips tightened.

"I'll call you later," he said, his voice low.

"Why don't I call *you*. I have a ton of work ahead of me." She moved away to gather her team.

Lexington moved through the spaces, floor by floor, at least where they had access, and pointed out specific areas and their location on the design plans to Ashanti and Nia. It was good that she had her laptop with the virtual layout because her mind was still on Monty and that woman. It was clear that she was a helluva lot more than just a television whatever. There was something between them—the way she touched him, the way he looked at her, the way she called him *Monty*. What businessperson would feel so comfortable to call him Monty—if it was only business? That was a name used by those who knew him personally—*intimately*. It was the name she cried out when he kissed the inside of her thighs, stroked her spine, made her orgasm all over him time and again.

"Lexi… Ms. Randall…"

Lexington blinked. Nia came into focus. "Sorry." She gave a short shake of her head.

"I was asking if we were done. I took plenty of notes and Ti has some great shots of the spaces."

She looked around as if seeing where she was standing for the first time. "Uh, yes. I think we've seen enough," she said over a tight smile.

They'd been able to get only as far as the fourth floor as the upper levels had too much construction underway. When they returned to the lobby the camera crew was gone and so was Montgomery. Her thoughts swirled into a dangerous storm. She removed her hard hat.

Sterling strolled over. "Lexington, I didn't get a chance to say hello earlier. Get everything you needed?" Even as he spoke to her, his gaze kept shifting to Ashanti.

"Actually, yes. I didn't know that there was going to be a television segment…"

"Yeah, just kinda came up." He gave a slight shrug. "We thought it would be a great opportunity to get to talk about not only this project but the kind of rehabilitation we're doing throughout the district."

"That sounds…fantastic. People need to know about the good work that MG Holdings is doing." She wanted to probe him about that woman, Stella. She knew how close Monty and Sterling were, more best friends and brothers, than merely cousins and business partners. But she wasn't going to be *that* kind of woman, picking intel from relatives. It would be up to Monty to tell her what the deal was, even as much as she was itching to ask Sterling just what the hell was going on between them. Besides, nonchalant was the move. If she knew nothing else, Monty would certainly ask Sterling what she'd said, how she'd acted. Inwardly she smiled. He would have nothing of substance to report.

"Good seeing you, Sterling. I'm going to head back."

"Sure. Sure. Good seeing you, too. Everyone is anxious to see what you can do with the joint once all of this—" he gave an expansive wave of his hand "—is done. Nice meeting the new members of the team, by the way. Stop by anytime." He flashed a soft smile in Ashanti's direction who bit down on her bottom lip and tried not to grin.

"I'm certain we will," Lexington said. "Take care, Sterling." She and Nia started for the door. When they emerged outside, Ashanti had yet to join them.

"I'll put my notes together and have them for you in the morning if that's okay."

"Of course."

"I have to wait for Ti. No need for you to hang around."

Lexington gave a short nod, glanced once at the door.

"Sure. I'll see you all tomorrow. We can do our Zoom meeting around noon to recap. Let Ashanti know," she said with a wave, and then walked to her car.

By the time she'd driven back home, she'd had enough time to let go of the green streak and put things in perspective. Almost. If she was honest with herself the last person that should have an issue with "not telling the whole story" was her. But her experience with all the men in her life had left her wary, skeptical of motives and intent. There was a part of her that believed that if the opportunity or the necessity presented itself she would be betrayed by the very men who swore they cared.

So, if Montgomery had a story to tell, she would listen. But if today was any indication of the road she was heading down with Montgomery, with her emotions as signposts, she didn't want any part of it. She wouldn't be hurt again. That was not an option. And the only way to prevent that was not to let anyone in and never let her feelings out.

"Where'd you go?" Sterling asked, wedging his cell phone between his jaw and shoulder. He pulled open his car door.

"Man, I don't even know how I wound up saying yes."

"Say what? Say yes. What the hell, man—"

"Whoa. Not *that* kind of say yes. She asked me to come over to the studio and talk with the head of the division and the other producers on the segment."

"I told you I needed to be your wingman. You should

have said something. I would have gone with you. So that's all it was, a meeting?"

"Yes. Totally. Everything was very professional and aboveboard."

"Awright. So when is the interview?"

"They're working out the details and the studio schedule. Should know something in about a week or so."

"Cool."

"In light of total transparency, she did invite me over to her new place—again."

Sterling turned the key in the ignition. "I hope you put a lock and key on that."

"I did. Look, it was all kinds of awkward this afternoon with Lexi showing up like that."

Sterling scoffed. "Ya think?"

"Did you get to talk to her?"

"Yep."

"Sooo…"

"So what?"

"Yo man, you gonna make me beg?"

Sterling relented and recounted his conversation with and the demeanor of Lexington. "Feel better now?" he asked, teasing.

"Somewhat. I'm going to head home, shower, change and go over to her place. See if I can make it up to her—explain."

"You ready to tell her all the details about you and Stella?"

"As much as she needs to know."

"Hey, your life. Do what you think is best. But on a side note, did you meet the sister with the locs?"

Montgomery chuckled. "Yes, you mean Ashanti, I presume."

"Yeah, yeah."

"What about her, Sterling?" he asked with a hint of warning in his tone.

"I think I might want to get to know her—outside of work. It was weird. I saw her and when she looked at me I felt like—" he paused "—I don't know. I can't explain it."

Montgomery full out laughed this time. "I. Do. Not. Believe. What. I'm. Hearing."

"Aw come on, man." He snorted a laugh. "Can happen to the best of us."

"Apparently. Well, look, I'm gonna tell you like you tell me. Think with your head. Don't let a relationship interfere with work. And treat her decently no matter what."

"That's the plan."

"Okay," he said on a breath. "Good luck. And cuz, if none of that works let your heart be your guide." He clapped him on the shoulder.

"Yeah, thanks. See you in the office tomorrow."

"Later."

Montgomery stepped out of the steamy shower. He used a hand towel to wipe the mist from the mirror. He checked his jaw for the late-day stubble, decided he could forgo a shave until morning.

He'd been debating with himself for the whole ride home if he should call her first or just show up? If he called she could say no. If he showed up she could... He didn't want to think that she was seeing anyone—but she just might not let him in or even be home.

He padded into his bedroom and picked up his cell from where he'd tossed it on the bed. *To call or not to call, that is the question.* He chuckled to himself, feeling like a confused teen. He scrolled for her number and listened to it ring.

"Hello?"

There was noise in the background, like machines.

"Hi, Lexi. It's me, Monty."

"Hold on," she shouted. "I can't really hear you."

By degrees the noise seemed to recede.

"Sorry, I was out back. My father was trying out his new lawnmower."

"Oh. Um, I was thinking if you were finally unbusy, I could stop by."

Silence.

"Hello?"

"Fine."

Oh, damn. His stomach rose and fell. He hated that word. He cleared his throat. "What time works for you?"

"Seven."

"Cool. I'll see you at seven."

"Fine."

The call ended.

Montgomery squeezed his eyes shut. He needed to be on his A game.

"Dad!" Lexington called out over the roar of the motor. She waved her arms over her head to get his attention.

He cut the engine and took off his headphones.

"Montgomery Grant is going to stop by around seven. To talk about the project. I thought you'd want to join us."

He didn't reply.

"I'm going to pull something together for dinner," she said, hooking her finger over her shoulder toward the house.

He lifted his hand in acknowledgement and turned the motor back on.

She let the screen door slam behind her and wondered for the zillionth time since she'd been back, why she bothered to say anything. It was clear that, sink or swim, what was left of Randall Architect and Design was totally on her shoulders.

After seasoning the chicken to roast, she sat at the kitchen table and flipped through the mail. She stopped short when her gaze landed on an envelope with a registered mail label on it. Her pulse quickened while she ripped open the envelope.

It was a court document that one of the vendors had legally begun the process to attach a lien on the house. She had forty-five days to either pay in full or go to court and fight it.

She spewed a stream of curses. Read the letter again and cursed some more. She snatched up the letter and stormed back outside to confront her father.

She marched right up to him and snatched the headphones off his head.

"Lexi, what is wrong with you?"

She waved the letter in front of his face. "This! This is what's wrong with me. It's not bad enough that you and Max stiffed half our contractors and vendors, now one of them has started actions to put a lien on the house! It's no longer a threat, Dad, this is real."

He wiped his brow with the back of his hand. At least he had the good sense to look chastised. "I'm sure we can work something out."

"Something out! Do you hear yourself? Work something out means that they need to be paid. If this goes public, it will tank the business totally and we could lose our home. Don't you get it?" She heard her voice rising above the treetops but she couldn't stop herself.

"Lexi... I turned all the finances over to your brother when I stepped back from the business. He was supposed to handle all that. Take care of everything."

She almost felt sorry for him. But not quite. "Obviously that's not what happened." She pressed her hand to her head. "I've been going over the records. What I'm seeing is not making sense."

He frowned as if thinking of what ridiculous thing he could say to her next, but didn't say a word.

She stared at her father for a long moment, then spun away and stormed back inside.

She heard her father's Jeep pull out of the driveway moments before the doorbell rang. Just as well, she reasoned. At least her fury had time to reduce to a simmer. She wiped her hands on a dish towel and went to the door ready to unleash the remnants of her anger on Montgomery.

She tugged the door open, but when she saw him standing there fine as all get-out, in a fitted black T-shirt and black jeans, smelling so good, and just enough shadow on his jaw to give him an even more rugged look, she felt something go soft inside. But he wouldn't get off that easy.

"Come in," she said, with as much chill in her voice as she could summon to disguise the rise of longing she felt. What she wanted to do was walk into his arms and set all her worries aside. What she did instead was leave him standing in the doorway while she walked through the house to the kitchen.

Montgomery followed.

"We need to talk," he said to her back.

She almost stopped at the fateful line. Her heart thumped. *That's never good.* She settled her expression and turned to face him. "Fine." She pulled out a chair at the kitchen table and sat. "I was just finishing dinner. Are you planning to stay or is this a short conversation?" Her stomach was in knots.

"I'd love to stay for dinner—if you want me to."

She lifted her chin. "Up to you. There's plenty."

He lowered his gaze and licked his bottom lip, then looked her right in the eyes, catching her off guard.

"I should have said something about the television thing."

She gave a shrug. "None of my business." She leaned on her elbow and propped her chin in her hand.

"I didn't say anything because…there's a history between me and Stella. I guess I wasn't sure what to say."

She sputtered a laugh. "We're adults, Monty. I didn't expect that you were some kind of monk before we met." Her heart was beating so fast she could barely breathe. Looking at him struggling to find the words to let her down easy, all she could think about was that he would simply be added to the line of men that had betrayed her in some way. Yet this time she thought it would be different. She'd been naïve enough to let her guard down a little too low and Monty leaped right over it and into her heart. Mentally she'd begun preparing herself for what it would be like when she went back to Paris. She concocted myriad scenarios of them being international lovers, meeting in slow motion in airports and train stations. She thought she'd stopped being so gullible after Gabriel. *Old habits die hard. Just say it. Say it's over so that I can refocus and put you in the rearview. I've done it before, I can do it again.*

"It's not that simple."

The words broke through the dark turn her thoughts had taken her. She blinked. "What's not so simple?"

He reached across the table and took her hand. "Just hear me out, okay?"

Her insides quivered. "Fine. I'm listening."

"Stella and I..."

Slowly and deliberately he told her about his relationship with Stella; how it began at a book signing years earlier. They'd sat next to each other at Mahogany Bookstore during a reading by Isabel Wilkerson discussing her book *The Warmth of Other Suns*. They'd talked afterward, standing behind each other on line to have their copies signed and they kept talking and walking late into the night, both sharing their passion for the revitalization of the place they called home. It was difficult at times, he'd said, as her job put her on the road for weeks on end. But they made it work. Until it didn't.

Lexington's heart ached and broke into tiny pieces when he haltingly but deliberately told her what Stella had done, how she'd done it and what it did to him, how she'd tried to explain and rationalize her reasons. Now she was back.

She squeezed his hand between her own.

He looked directly at her. "There's nothing between us, Lexi. Nothing. I couldn't go back even if I wanted to, and I don't. This thing with the television station may be her way to 'make up' for something." He shrugged. "But in the end it will only help spotlight the kind of work I'm doing. And that's all that matters."

She pulled in a long breath, braced herself for the answer to her question; did she want him back?

"Yes." He rocked his jaw. "She's invited me to her new place—which in light of total transparency my company helped her find—and out for drinks."

"And?"

"I've told her no—every time." He slipped his hand out of her grip and reached up to cup her chin. "I told her no because of you. You're the one that I want for however long this thing lasts between us. As long as you want it to. Tell me you do." He moved closer. His gaze locked onto hers holding her in place. "Tell me," he urged.

She wanted to say yes, give in. Hadn't he all but told her that he really cared about her? She shouldn't blame him for holding secrets. She had secrets of her own. But hers were different.

She nodded her head. "Yes," she whispered over the rush of conflicting emotions whipping through her.

Montgomery leaned in and kissed her, softly at first as if to test the waters then with more urgency as she yielded to him, turned herself over to him; the taste of him, the feel of him sweeping her away as it always did.

But she would never tell him that, never expose how vulnerable he made her feel. Not now. Maybe never.

Montgomery lay with her in her soft-as-cloud bed, her head resting on his chest. There was a certain kind of comfort in listening to the even pace of her breathing, the steady beat of her heart against his chest. He closed his eyes, replaying like a movie director frame by frame how the evening had progressed. When he'd stood in her doorway he had no way of knowing if she'd even listen to him. All he could do was hope. Then when she did he wasn't certain if he could tell her everything, the depths of the hurt he'd felt. But he had, and she listened. She'd held his hand and fought back her own tears and she listened. And when they made love he almost allowed himself to believe that this could work beyond the boundaries that they'd given themselves. Because as hard as it was, he could see that last frame of their movie with her saying goodbye and flying out of his life.

He kissed the top of her head. He couldn't become too invested. That would be a major mistake. Unfortunately, it was too late.

"Hmmm," she sighed, stretching and purring like a cat that had been thoroughly petted. "We should probably get up," she said lazily, before pressing her lips to his chest. "I didn't hear my father come back, but I'm sure it won't be much longer." She pulled herself to a sitting position and looked at him over her shoulder. "I'd hate for him to find a naked man in the house."

He raised up on his elbow. "Then come home with me."

She smiled. "Okay."

"I don't mean just for tonight. I mean…home with me until you're ready to leave."

His gaze sped back and forth across her face.

"I…" She frowned, studied him, looking for what she wasn't sure. "Are you asking me to move in with you?"

"We're together pretty much every night anyway. Then we don't have to concern ourselves with who's home and who isn't—except us." He stroked her thigh. "It can work." His brows tightened. "It's not forever. Just for now."

The last time she'd lived with a man, he'd brought her best friend home and had sex with her in the bed they'd shared. "I need to think about it."

He exhaled. "Cool. Think it over." He kissed her back and got out of bed, started gathering his discarded clothing. "Um, bathroom?"

She blinked. "Oh. Sorry." She got up, grabbed her robe and slipped it on while Monty put on his pants. "Down the hall on the right," she said, opening the bedroom door. "Clean towels are on the shelf…if you need anything," she said, feeling suddenly awkward and brand-new like a teenager sneaking around with the town bad boy.

"Thanks." He walked out.

Lexington flopped down on the bed, stared up at the ceiling. What the hell? He'd asked her to move in with him—albeit temporarily. He'd asked just the same. How crazy was that and how crazy would she be to accept such craziness? A couple of hours ago she was ready to hear the death knell of their passion-fueled relationship. Instead…

Her heart wanted to say yes. But her good sense told her no way. The warring factions whispered in her ear. Say yes. Say no.

The bedroom door opened. She popped up. Montgomery was fully dressed. He held a towel in his hand.

"I didn't know where to put this," he said.

She got up. "I'll take it. No worries."

He studied her. "You okay?"

She shifted her weight, put on a smile. "Yeah. I'm fine," she said, wishing she had pockets so she could do something with her hands.

He leaned down and kissed her. "I can let myself out." He turned away and walked down the stairs.

Lexington listened to the front door open and close, the sound of his car engine start up and finally fade. Her gaze moved slowly around her room. The room she'd returned to time and again through the years even as an adult. She walked over to the window, pushed the curtain aside. Heavy clouds blotted out the moon giving the sky an ethereal cast. She sat on the sill, where she'd sat so many nights, thinking, wishing, mapping out her life. Most of the time she figured things out. This time she felt lost, her thoughts obscured like the moon—there but indecipherable.

Sighing, she got to her feet, tightened the belt on her robe and went down to straighten up the kitchen. Maybe after a good night sleep, and sunshine in the morning, things would be clearer.

Three days went by. Days of mulling over and accepting and discarding decisions. Trying to stay focused on the daunting task of the project and the nerve-racking financial situation with the business. Her brother had been useless, telling her he was in Philly meeting with potential clients and they could talk when he got back in two weeks. After thoroughly cussing him out and getting no assistance from her father she finally made up her mind. It seemed so easy once she'd made the decision. What else could she have done?

Her heart was literally in her throat while she waited for an answer. She should have called first.

The door opened and Montgomery stood there, bare chested with a kitchen towel tossed over his shoulder. For a moment he simply stared at her as if suddenly he'd gazed into the sun. His eyes drifted down to the two suitcases at her feet, then rose to her face. A slow smile curved his lips.

"I, uh, heard you were in the market for a roommate," she said coyly.

"Do you want to know the terms of your lease?"

She took a step forward. "Why don't you give me all the details in the morning."

He chuckled and slid an arm around her waist, pulling her close. "Can I take your bags, ma'am?"

She looked into his eyes. "You can take anything you want," she whispered against his mouth.

Seven

They slipped into an easy routine, as if being under the same roof was as ordinary as the air they breathed. Montgomery's house had plenty of space. Enough for her to set up some office space where she could meet with Ashanti and Nia, work on the designs and unravel the company finances. She'd paid off half of the vendors and contractors, negotiated with Wilson & Sons, the company that was attempting the lien, to give her sixty days, and she was paying Ashanti and Nia who deserved every penny. The initial deposit from Monty was all but gone. While a large portion had gone for deposits for fabrics, paints, furnishings, she'd used a great deal of it to pay off the company debt. In the weeks ahead the balances would come due. Meanwhile she wasn't technically entitled to the next $100,000 until the job was a third of the way completed. They weren't there yet. She could go to Monty and ask for an advance on the balance. She could claim that there was an overrun in the cost of supplies. But then she'd find herself in the same situation as her father and brother.

"Hey, babe."

She glanced away from the computer screen. Monty was standing in the doorway.

"Hey." She leaned back in her seat. "You look edible."

He chuckled. "Not exactly the look I was going for. Heading over to the studio."

She pushed up from the chair and walked over to him. She adjusted his tie, leaned forward and kissed him lightly. "You're going to be a staarrr!" she said dramatically.

He kissed her. "See you later tonight. The show starts at eight. Figure we leave at six, grab a quick bite and head to the theater."

"Sounds perfect. I'll be ready."

"And I can't wait to see you at the end of my day." He kissed her again then hurried off.

"Break a leg!" she called out. She leaned for a moment against the door frame and wrapped her arms around her waist, realizing in that moment just how happy she was, despite all the shadows that loomed around her. Montgomery was that light, the bright spot at the end of the dark tunnel beckoning her.

She turned back to her desk. She needed to check in with Danielle and the progress on the project in Paris. An hour later she hung up with Danielle, satisfied that everything was under control and a potential new project was being floated to her business. Just as she started to get up from the desk, her cell rang. It was Nia.

"Nia. Hi."

"Hello, Lexi. Um, I'm not generally one to read the gossip columns but your name has come up."

"My name?" she asked, incredulous.

"Yes. The headline is Playboy Real Estate Mogul Entangled with Faux Heiress."

"What!" She leaped to her feet. Her heart was racing. She began to pace. "Which paper?"

"The *Washington Times*."

"Okay. I'll read it. I'm sure there's some mistake." She squeezed her eyes shut.

"There's more."

Lexington lowered herself into the chair at her desk. "Tell me."

"It's on the internet. People are already talking."

She started to feel ill. "Thank you for letting me know," she murmured.

"Is there anything I can do?"

"No."

"I think it's important that you think about a statement in the event that you're contacted by the media. This project has gotten a lot of attention over the past few months. We would need to be ready."

"Of course."

"I, uh, hate to ask this, but is there any truth to what they're saying, that the company is under water, bordering on bankruptcy, in debt to dozens of vendors?"

There was no point in hiding the truth any longer. "Can you come by? I'll give Ashanti a call. I should talk to you both together."

* * *

She jumped every time she heard a car drive by. Ashanti and Nia had been gone for a while. She'd been honest with them, laying out the reason why she came back, the truth about Randall finances, her family mismanagement, the debt and what her plan had been to set the ship right. She explained as best she could why she'd hidden the truth. She needed to get around the curve and see some daylight first, get the company back on solid ground. There was no way a project as big as Essex House would have taken her on otherwise. All she'd needed was time to work it all out. She assured them both that their employment was secure. They had her word.

Before they'd left Nia had asked to speak with her. She told her that she believed in her, was awed by her work and vision and wanted to help. She admitted that the reason why she was so good with management was that she had an undergrad degree in forensic accounting. She offered to dig into Randall Architect and Design accounts and see if she could find what Lexington missed. If Lexington wanted her to. Things couldn't be worse so she agreed, grateful for the help. She had very strong suspicions of what was going on, but she simply could not find it. Hopefully Nia could. In the meantime, she had to face Montgomery.

If there was any mercy in the world, she would have the chance to explain everything to Montgomery before he heard it elsewhere. That was not to be.

Montgomery was so angry that his hand shook as he brought the tumbler of bourbon to his lips. "I don't believe this mess," he fumed to his cousin, then spewed another train of expletives.

"Hey, man, I feel responsible for this. I should have looked harder at the business."

Montgomery stared glumly into his glass. "Not on you. I gave you the seal of approval. I let my libido lead me by the nose. Dammit." He slammed his fist on the table rattling the contents. "She freaking lied to me. From the beginning. And when do I find out? In the middle of a television interview!" He snorted a laugh. "I'd swear Stella looked like she was enjoying every minute of it, even while she was playing sympathetic. *How could you have not known,*" he singsonged, mimicking Stella. *"Is this Lexington Randall even competent to do the work? This is such an important project to get possibly derailed by a financial scandal."* He finished his drink and poured another, well on his way to totally numbing his disbelief, hurt and anger that roared through him in surging waves.

"Before you're too wasted to have a conversation we need to figure out what we're going to do. This time tomorrow, the other papers will be all over this. The only leg up is that the session was recorded. Maybe you can talk Stella into not airing it or heavily edit it to buy us some time."

Montgomery groaned. He looked across at his cousin. "Why would she do this? Lie to me? Move in with me. Look me in the face day after day and know this whole thing was all smoke and mirrors."

"You're going to have to talk to her."

He shook his head. "What's to talk about? She used me. Used my company to shore up her own failing business!"

"Listen, we both looked at the same information. I admit I fell down on my end. I only did a surface scan of the company background. But, for real, she has skills, man. That's not up for debate. She's damn good at what she does. She can still do the job."

"Still do the job! Are you kidding? I don't want her within a hundred yards of me and that project."

Sterling leaned in. "Let's be honest, Monty. We are way too far in to have her pull out now. She's implementing the designs with the contractors, negotiating with damn near all our suppliers." He raised his hands up in defeat. "I don't see how we can do it and not throw the entire project months behind schedule."

Montgomery heaved a weary sigh. "Don't have any choice, man. I'm done. If she'd lie to me like this, build up this whole imaginary world to win me over, what the hell else would she do? It was all about money." He sputtered a nasty laugh. "Money."

"So what are you going to do? The project cannot afford to start over."

Montgomery wrapped his hands around his glass. "The first thing is to have her leave my house." Saying the words broke something in him. "We'll figure out what to do about the job." He struggled to swallow over the hard knot in his throat.

He grimaced as the spare bedroom ceiling in Sterling's house spun. He'd ignored her calls and text messages, knowing that anything he said in his current mindset he'd regret or maybe not and that was worse. He hoped that with a dawning of a new day he'd have it worked out. He didn't.

* * *

When he put the key in the door and stepped across the threshold, he wasn't sure what he'd hoped for or expected.

Lexington stood from her place on the couch. She didn't flinch, appear contrite, or even combative. Her expression was one of clear resolve, as if unlike him, she'd spent the night envisioning this moment.

"My bags are already in the car. I'm sure that you want to know if what you've read is true." He watched her slender hand curl into a fist. "It is. I lied to you or at the very least covered it up. That's all that's important. The reasons are only excuses, and I've never been in the business of offering excuses for what I do." She paused, lifted her chin. "Whatever we had…obviously can't continue. However, whatever you might think or believe of me, I'm damned good at my job. The best. You know that. Everything is in place for the work to continue. I'd like to see this project to completion. Ashanti and Nia are totally competent. I will work remotely, overseeing the progress on our end." She hesitated, the first time she seemed uncertain. "That way you… We won't have to interact."

She picked up her tote from the couch and adjusted the strap over her shoulder. She walked purposefully toward the door. When she stopped in front of him, for the first time he saw a flicker of pain in the water that momentarily clouded her eyes before being blinked away.

"I'm sorry, Monty," she said softly, then walked past him and out.

He kept his back to the outside until he heard her car pull off. Finally he closed the door. Her scent still lingered in the air. He tossed his phone onto the couch, paced, ran his hand across his face as if he could somehow wipe all the mess away.

Suddenly he started to laugh. It just bubbled up from his gut and tumbled out into the room. Damn, she really was good. She was five moves ahead, having already foreseen any attack he might throw at her. He couldn't accuse her of lying. She admitted she lied. No point in coming up with reasons since they were only excuses. She admitted that. He couldn't say she wasn't qualified. She totally was. He couldn't tell her to get out. She was already leaving.

"Damn." He shook his head. Slowly he sobered. It might be momentarily amusing how the past few moments went down, but the reality was that she'd done something to him that he'd sworn he wouldn't let happen again—allow himself to become vulnerable to a woman that would set him up for this raw emotion of pain. To take him out of himself. That could not be forgiven.

Lexington was right. Sterling was right. It was too late to start over. All that was left was damage control. Craft his own narrative.

She could barely see in front of her from the tears that continued to fill her eyes and slide down her cheeks. She sniffed. Wiped. Sniffed. Slammed her palm on the steering wheel. The lid had blown off the pot. Everything was boiling over. Spilling. Making one big mess. That's what her life had become.

She should have never returned to DC. From the moment she got the call from her father she should have known better. But, as always, trying to please, trying to win her father's heart and respect, she'd come back. And to compound an already-shaky situation, she'd covered up the truth in order to save her family business and now they would pay for it. Dammit, what was she thinking!

A string of car horns blared behind her. She glanced up at the green light. Gave a shake of her head and cut across the intersection.

What was even more heartbreaking than the treatment she received from her father and her brother was the pain she knew she'd inflicted on Montgomery. He'd trusted her. He'd opened his heart and his home to her. And she'd betrayed him. The very thing she'd experienced and abhorred in others. She had to make it right.

Pulling into the driveway of her family home, with suitcases in tow, only intensified her fury and humiliation. Crawling back. That's what it felt like. She could easily blame her father and brother but she was as much at fault as they were.

She parked behind her father's Jeep, took her bags from the trunk and went inside.

Her father was in the kitchen fixing a cup of coffee. He looked totally taken aback seeing her standing in the archway of the kitchen.

"Lexi…everything okay?"

"No, Dad. Everything is not okay. I need you to sit down. We're going to have a talk."

More than an hour later Lexington had laid out everything that she'd done since her arrival in order to save the family business, a business that only she was interested in saving. She'd lied. She'd hurt the man she was falling in love with. She'd created this image of a solvent company and it all backfired. She didn't care how it affected her, but how it affected Montgomery, his standing and reputation in the community. She'd shown her father one of the headlines from an online news site saying how a *faux heiress duped the king of real estate.*

The only way she knew to fix it was to deliver on her promise of the vision for Essex House. But in the meantime, she informed her father, she was having Nia do a thorough deep dive into the company finances. She had her own suspicions, but she couldn't prove them. She'd worked out a deal with the lien proceedings, and all but a handful of the old vendors had been paid in full. Once the company was fully stabilized, and her job with Essex House completed, she was returning to her life and business in Paris, and warned her father never to call her about Randall Architect and Design ever again.

She pushed to her feet. "All I ever wanted was your love and respect. To *see* me and to embrace the dreams I had for myself. You could never do that. You only saw Maxwell, tried to shape him into something he could never be, never wanted to be and it crippled him and nearly destroyed this business in the process. And for what, Daddy, just so that you could say you turned the family business over to your *son*?"

She blinked furiously to stem the tears before she whirled away, too quick to hear her father's whispered words, *"What have I done?"*

* * *

Lexington held a virtual meeting with Ashanti and Nia. She informed them that because of the bad publicity she was going to take a back seat. And although she would give final approvals, she would not be on the site at any point from there on. They would handle all the onsite work going forward. If they were contacted by the media, they were to simply say that they were there to do a job and that's it. No further comment. She held her breath waiting to hear their response.

Ashanti and Nia agreed without question to the plan going forward and shared their commitment and solidarity to her. They had her back.

Lexington silently sighed in relief. With that hard task aside, she ran a hot bath and poured in her favorite lavender bath salts. Immersed beneath the steamy water, she leaned her head back against the lip of the tub and wept.

It had been more than a week since that morning. Even as he moved with precision through the myriad tasks of running his businesses, his thoughts never strayed far enough away from Lexington to allow him to sleep at night, not see her in the reflection of store windows, hear her throaty laughter or shake the feel of her body curled next to his. He vacillated between anger and pain and back again.

"You look like crap."

He glanced up at Sterling and looked away.

Sterling came in and sat down without asking. "You talk to her?"

"Who?" he asked, knowing perfectly well who Sterling meant.

"Lexington."

"No. We said all that needed to be said."

"Hmm. That's why you look like death warmed over."

"I'm handling it. Stella is on her way here now. I'm going to see if she can either edit out the portion of the interview or…something."

"I hate to say I told you so, but Stella was trouble from the moment she set foot back in your life."

"It's *her* fault that Lexington Randall is a liar?" he snapped.

"Whoa!" He held up his hands. "The transformation is complete."

"What the hell does that mean?"

"It means that Stella has somehow turned you to the dark side, actually defending her."

"I'm not defending her," he said, none too convincingly.

"Yeah. Right. Look, man, do what you think is best, just don't sell your soul. Stella wants you back. It's been clear from the beginning and if she can use this interview, and the PR mess to do it, she will. I guarantee it."

"I think you're giving her too much diabolical credit," he said only half joking.

"Say what you want but I stand by my conviction." He pushed out a breath and stood. "Uh, I know that things went sideways with you and Lexington, but I'm hoping you won't have an issue with me seeing Ashanti, her assistant."

The corner of Montgomery's mouth curved and he

chuckled. "No, bruh. Be happy. Only thing I ask is that you do me the courtesy and give a heads-up if Lexi is going to be in the vicinity."

"Will do." He checked his Rolex. "I have to meet with Gabriel in like fifteen minutes. I want to go over some of the construction projections."

Montgomery nodded. "Let me know whatever I need to know," he said with a half smile.

Once Sterling was gone, Montgomery decided he needed a short stroll to get his circulation moving and lift the fog from his brain.

"I'll be back in about ten minutes," he told Cherise. "Ms. Vincent isn't due for about an hour but if she arrives before I do just have her wait in the conference room."

"Sure thing."

When he stepped outside it really hit him that summer was in full swing. Sundresses, sandals, T-shirts and shorts had become the outfits of the day; the businessmen were jacketless, ties loosened and top buttons undone as they wove their way along the crowded streets and in and out of diners and restaurants in search of a quick lunch. And like with just about every thought, feeling or new realization, images of Lexington accompanied them. He saw the two of them hand in hand taking in the sun and the sights. Happy.

He bumped headlong into a couple, startling them all. He apologized profusely before continuing down the street chastising himself for being so distracted— by thoughts of Lexington. He turned the corner and decided to run into the coffee shop for an iced tea. While he waited on line for his order he took in the space, the long counter lined with customers, and circular tables dotted with lunch goers. He inched up on the line when he frowned in confusion at what he saw.

At a back table Stella was seated opposite Gabriel in what appeared to be a very intense conversation. There was probably a laundry list of reasons for them to be there together. He couldn't think of any off the top of his head.

Gabriel lifted his cell phone from the table and checked, said something to Stella who nodded.

"Next."

Montgomery blinked and stepped forward to place his order. He kept looking across the room. Gabriel was getting up. Stella reached out and squeezed his hand before moving to leave.

"Hey, Gabe," he called out as Gabriel reached the door.

Gabriel stopped and when he turned the look of surprise could not have been more evident. His eyes darted to Stella then back. He grinned. "Heading over to the office to meet with Sterling," he said above the heads and shoulders of the customers.

"Yeah. He told me. Catch up with you later."

"Sure." He gave a short nod and left.

"$3.75," the clerk said, handing Montgomery his iced tea.

He paid for his purchase and walked over to where Stella was seated. "Didn't know you and my project manager were friendly." He pulled out a chair.

"Good afternoon to you too, Monty," she said with a smile. "We aren't friends. Just happened to run into each other. Have a seat. Since you're here we can talk now or go to the office, whichever you prefer."

He sat. "I'll get straight to the point," he said. "I really need you to hold off on airing that interview or at least take out the section about Ms. Randall's company."

She pursed her lips sympathetically and sighed. "I really can't do that. The taping is being edited as we speak. It's scheduled to air next week."

"That can't happen. You do realize that your two minutes of fame could torpedo a major project for the community?"

Her eyes widened at the barb. "You think that's what I'm after? Fame?" She scoffed. "You really don't know me, do you?"

"Actually no. I don't."

Her features pinched. "What I might be able to do is a prerecorded piece that pretty much exonerates you and puts the onus on *her* for this mess. It can be added to the end of the interview. Sort of a follow-up." She paused. "What do you think?"

Was slinging mud at Lexi and ruining what might be left of her integrity what he really wanted to do?

"Listen, think about it. We still have some time. We can spin this thing. I'm sure that if we put our heads together we can work something out. The last thing I want to do is screw anything up for you. I think it'll be important for everyone to know that someone of your stature didn't get taken in by a pretty face. It would totally ruin your brand."

He stared at her from across the table, and what he saw in her eyes was totally unsettling.

She smiled in invitation. "I still have an unopened

bottle of wine that I was hoping to share with you to christen my new place." She bit down on her bottom lip.

"Don't think that would be a good idea, Stella." He pushed to his feet.

"I think it would be…" She gave a light shrug. "But I understand." She looked up at him. "In the meantime, think about spinning the message like I suggested and get back to me before the end of the week." She covered his hand with hers. "I want to help, Monty."

He eased his hand out of her hold. "I'll keep that in mind." He walked out, more concerned than before that the "leak" about Lexington was no accident.

When he returned to the office he instructed Cherise to get in touch with the company attorney, then he had a conversation with Sterling.

It took a few days and the pulling of several strings, but the corporate attorney for MG Holdings, Montgomery's frat brother Xavier Coster, was able to get a temporary injunction to halt the airing of the segment on Essex House. The accommodating judge had managed to set a court date for six months from the date of the filing—which was when his schedule would be clear. By then, Montgomery and Sterling concluded, the project would be ready for the grand opening and the segment wouldn't matter any longer.

With the weight of the television problem out of the way, Montgomery could focus his attention where he wanted it, on the completion of Essex House. He'd hired a social media–savvy tech whiz to mitigate any debris about Essex House and Randall Architect and Design issues, and in a matter of a couple of weeks, Essex House was trending for all the right reasons. Progress images were posted regularly on every social media platform and the project was continually touted as the new Second Coming for the district. However, Cara Mack, his social media magician had advised him to stay out of the limelight and not to accept any offers for quotes or interviews until the project was complete. The last thing they needed was to have the story and questions dredged up. People loved nothing better than some good gossip, but fortunately the attention span was short, and she guaranteed folks would move on to the next hot topic.

Construction continued at a steady pace and day by day what was once a shell of a building was transformed into the gem he'd envisioned. All the electrical and plumbing had been completed and signed off on by the inspectors, with everything being above code. If there was one thing that Montgomery was adamant about it was the safety and security of the building and everyone who lived or worked there. He made sure only the best materials were used, and there was no scrimping to save money. He'd known of too many projects that looked all shiny and new, but were made with crappy materials, that fell apart with minimal use—and building codes were the bare minimum to cut corners. That's not what he wanted. The high quality, glitz and glamour of Essex House would be for real. The apartments, office spaces, recreation rooms and restaurant were framed, high quality insulation installed, plaster walls put up that would take a truck to knock down, and real wood floors laid throughout.

The shipments with the furnishings, window dressings, paints and appliances had begun to arrive. Ashanti and Nia were on site every day giving directions to the shippers to ensure that everything was placed exactly where it should.

Montgomery stopped by to inspect the property at least three times per week, secretly in the hopes of seeing Lexi. But she was never there, and he wouldn't ask her assistants where or how she was, although he could probably find out from Sterling who seemed to spend all of his free time with Ashanti. He wouldn't do that either. The least he could do was respect her decision to cut ties. After all, it was her deception that got them to this place.

That's the line he fed himself, to console himself and beat back his longing for her. Whatever it was, he was sure now, more clearheaded, that she had her reasons—not excuses but reasons. They needed to talk. Well—he needed to talk to her.

He pulled his cell phone out of his pocket, just as his intercom buzzed.

"Yes, Cherise?"

"Mr. Grant, Ms. Vincent is here to see you."

He closed his eyes and inwardly groaned. Since the injunction she'd done everything short of sending in SWAT to get him to talk to her. Her messages vacillated between anger to tears, to outrage to contrition and back again. He couldn't avoid a face-to-face forever.

"Thanks, Cherise," he finally said. "Send her in." He steeled himself for whatever barrage she lobbed his way.

Moments later his door opened.

When he stood to greet her he was again stunned

by how pretty she was, how sweet she could be. For an instant his stance softened. For an instant.

"Stella."

She crossed the room, not with her usual take over the world strut but hesitant almost.

"Mind if I sit down?"

"Please do." He returned to his seat, leaned back in his seat and waited.

She fidgeted with the purse on her lap then finally looked across at him. "I'm sorry. About everything." She sniffed. "Seems like that's all I do when it comes to us—I mean—you. Apologize."

"What are you apologizing for, Stella?"

She tugged in a breath. "I never had to use the information I got about Randall Architect and Design."

He sat up a bit straighter.

"I saw how you looked at her that day. I remember that look, Monty. You used to look at me like that." She paused. "I wanted it again." Her lips trembled. "So when Gabe Martin came to me—"

He jerked forward. "Wait. What did you say? Gabe Martin?"

She nodded. "At first it was just flirting. We went to dinner…and one evening he told me about Randall's financial troubles and how he didn't understand how you would get involved with a company that was falling apart. He said he had a friend who'd worked with them and had gotten stiffed, along with others." She took a breath. "I should have come to you, asked you first instead of springing it on you, then holding it over your head." She sniffed and dabbed at her eye. "I let jealousy blind me. I wanted you to see that she wasn't right for you, and it was the way I found to do it. And I'm sorry." She rose to her feet. "Your little injunction stunt cost me big points at my job," she said with a soft smile. "But I charmed my way back."

"I'm sure you did." He slowly stood and came around his desk. He looked into her upturned face and again wondered how things had gone so completely wrong between them. But he guessed at the end of the day they were not meant to be together. Simple as that. "Thank you for coming here and telling me, Stella."

She leaned up and kissed his cheek then dabbed the lipstick away with her thumb. "Take care, Monty."

"You, too."

She walked toward the door, stopped and turned back. "I know you don't owe me any favors, but I'm hoping that you will let me film the grand opening. I'll be on my best behavior."

He slid his hands into the pockets of his slacks and half smiled. "The invitation is open."

She grinned and walked out.

Standing in the middle of his office he wasn't sure what he should do first, call Lexi or fire Gabe.

There was a light knock on his door.

"Yes. Come in."

"This just came for you, by messenger," Cherise said, handing him an envelope.

"Thanks," he mumbled. He opened the envelope and inside was an embossed thank-you card from Randall Architect and Design.

He opened the card and read the script in Lexington's neat handwriting.

Dear Mr. Grant,

Thank you for the opportunity to work on such
an important project. I am sure you will continue
to do great things for your community. We wish
you much success.

Sincerely,
Lexington Randall

He read the card three times. It wasn't so much that
she'd sent a thank-you card that threw him; it was the
cold, distant tone that shouted at him from the ivory
paper. His question about what to do first was answered.

For several moments Montgomery sat behind the
wheel of his car contemplating all the scenarios that
could play out in the next few minutes. It could go either
way, congenial or contentious. The choice was not his.

He got out and walked the path to the front door.
The chime of the bell softly pinged beyond the door. He
dragged in a breath just as the door opened.

Lexington Randall, Sr. stood in the door. His smooth
brown face creased in question. "Mr. Grant. Something
wrong?"

He cleared his throat. "I was hoping to speak with
your daughter."

"Oh," he chortled. "Lexi's not here. Been gone about
two weeks now."

Montgomery's stomach knotted. "Gone? She
moved?" he asked, figuring she'd finally had her fill
of living at home.

"You could say that. Uh, you want to come in, son? I have a pot on the stove."

"Just for a moment."

Lexington Sr. stepped aside to let Montgomery in then walked to the kitchen.

"Was fixing some chicken stew." He chuckled. "Last all week. Won't have to cook. Gets to be a bit much cooking every day for one person. Something to drink?"

"Uh, no. Thanks. Do you have Lexi's address?"

"I'll write it down for you." He turned from the stove and studied Montgomery for a moment.

"Thought you would have been the one," he said quietly.

"Sir?"

"I know Lexi figured I didn't know or didn't care. But I knew. I saw the look in her eyes when she mentioned your name. When she said she was gonna be staying with you I thought for sure she'd settle down, be happy again. Stay." He wiped his hands on a small blue and white towel. "Then she came back here."

Montgomery flinched.

"The light had gone out of her eyes and that hard edge was all around her again, like constantly bumping into the sharp side of a square table." He pulled out a chair and sat. "I blame you for that."

Montgomery opened his mouth to respond. Lexington held up his hand. "But I blame myself more. I didn't do right by my daughter, and it took the roof caving in and the pain in her eyes to make me see what a single-focused, last-generation fool I'd been." He gazed off into the distance. "When my wife, Grace, died, Lexi was only fifteen. She took on the role of caring for me and her brother. Cooked, cleaned, looked out for her brother, learned how to manage the household expenses and still remained at the top of her class. Had an eye for architecture and design since she was in grade school." He chuckled and shook his head at the memory. "But I didn't see it. Didn't want to really. I came from that old school where you turned the family business over to the son. I tried to force them into corners where they didn't belong. Max has skills but no head for the business and no interest. But no matter how often he showed me, I didn't want to see it." He sighed. "Lexi paid the price for my shortsightedness. And of course, who do I call when the manure hits the fan—my daughter—and she came. And she cleaned up our mess the way she's always done. I hurt my daughter and I will spend the rest of my life trying to make it up to her." He stared Montgomery hard in the eyes. "I may be a screwup. I can reconcile with that. But one thing I won't do is let someone else hurt her. I don't know what you did or what happened between the two of you, but I can tell you this much—Lexi's not gonna be the one to fix it. Not this time."

He pushed to his feet. "I'll get that address for you."

Eight

The cab squealed to a stop, jolting Montgomery to attention. He'd been a million miles away putting his thoughts into coherent sentences while trying to take in the scenery streaming by. Thankfully the taxi took credit cards. He paid his fare and stepped out in the balmy afternoon and into a quaint enclave that made him think he might be part of a time gone by. The buildings, stately yet inviting, were a testament to the mastery of their construction. The circular arrangement of almost mini communities included a private house, a short apartment building, a bakery and wine shop. He smiled, realizing now where the genesis for Essex House had come.

He checked the address against the piece of paper that Lexi's father had given him. There was a really good chance she wouldn't even be home, or worse that she wouldn't want to see him.

Two teenagers cruised by on bikes with brown paper bags strapped to their backs, bread tops poking out.

He approached the walkway of the three-story building just as the front door opened. Two women emerged, deep in animated conversation and at first he thought she would walk right by him, or cut across the grass and head in the opposite direction. But something made her look up. She stopped as suddenly as if she'd run into an invisible wall.

Slowly she took off her sunglasses.

The young woman touched her arm. Lexi nodded, said something to her and the woman walked off, throwing daggers over her shoulder at Montgomery.

He adjusted the weight of his duffle bag on his left shoulder. "Hello, Lexi." He didn't fully realize until that moment exactly how much he missed and needed her. It felt as if the weighty cloud that had hung around him since the day she left his house finally lifted. There was daylight, and it was Lexi.

Lexington's expression creased and uncreased as she tried to process what was happening. "What are you doing here? How did you even know where I was?"

"Your father."

She leaned her weight on her right hip. "I see, and you flew all the way to Paris to say hello?" She fought back a smile.

He gave a half shrug. "I was checking my passport and realized I'd never been to Paris...and you were here."

Her throat tightened. "Monty, I—"

"Wait, before you say anything." He took a step closer. "I love you, Lex. That's why I'm here. I'm here to tell you that I love you, and that there is no other woman who is as brilliant, as visionary, challenging, complex and shut-the-door sexy as you."

For all the nonchalant bravado she pretended to exhibit, her insides were mush. This was the second time that she'd run away after a bad relationship, but this time there was an alternate ending to her story. A happy one. One that included the man that she was crazy in love with, and she knew she'd never have to run again. She took a step closer. "Say that part again," she whispered.

Montgomery cupped her cheek. "Which part?"

"The part about me being brilliant." Her eyes sparked with mirth.

Montgomery tossed his head back and laughed long and deep, before he took her in his arms and kissed her, wiping away the hurt, the loneliness, the past and reigniting their future.

Reluctantly she eased back, but held on to him as if he might disappear as suddenly as he'd arrived. "How is this going to work, Monty? How can it? I have my business *here* and you have yours in DC."

The enormity of their reality settled over them.

"We can make it work. If we want to. I know I do."

A light sprinkling of rain began to fall.

She grabbed the lapels of his jacket. "Guess what?" she said against his lips.

"What?"

"I have my own place. No roomies. And I'd love to show you around."

He grinned. "Lead the way."

They'd barely crossed her threshold. Montgomery's bag dropped from his shoulder with a thud and they were in each other's arms. Jackets and sweaters were tugged off and tossed to the floor. They kissed and hugged and sought bare skin, leaving discarded clothes in their wake until finally tumbling onto her bed layered with thick pillows and a downy white comforter.

"We'll make it work," he vowed against her lips, easing down her body, planting hot, hungry kiss along satiny skin.

He kissed the swell of her breasts, the dip in her stomach, the curve between her thighs until she moaned and trembled beneath him.

Her fingertips pressed into his back, her legs wrapped around his waist. Like musical notes they came together in perfect harmony. That first push, that first sensation of being filled by him rolled through her in breath-stopping waves.

He groaned as she lifted her hips, turned them in slow, agonizing motion.

"I'm sorry about everything," she whispered.

He kissed away her apology and recommitted his love.

The intensity grew. Heat enveloped them. Pillows tumbled to the floor.

They moved together faster, harder, their need for release stealing the air from their lungs.

Lexington's head rolled back and forth. Her cry hung in her throat.

Montgomery reared up and sank deep inside that wet pulse of her walls, hurtling them to earth-rocking satisfaction.

"I love you, too," she cried as her body sucked out the last drops of him.

"It was my brother," she was saying against the dampness of his chest. "He was skimming money to launch his music production company. That's how the business started falling apart. And my father was so disconnected from what was going on…" She sighed.

"Damn. I'm sorry, baby." He stroked her hair away from her face. "How did you find out?"

"Nia." She half laughed. "The woman is good. She did her accounting magic and put the pieces together. I had it out with my brother, who played the 'woe is me' card. How he planned to put it all back once his business took off. Meanwhile I was left to clean up the mess." She blew out a breath. "I'm just glad to be done with the whole thing. I got everyone paid off, got the company back in the black. It will take work to get folks to trust the company again, but…after all it took to put it back together…" She sighed. "And then there's Nia and Ashanti… I hate the idea of just walking off, ya know, but I have my business here." Even to her own ears she heard the confusion. "I thought it would be easier to simply say goodbye to it all."

He sat up a bit, craned his neck to look at her. "I want to make an investment in your company. Be your part-

ner. We need black businesses to flourish. And I want
to be sure that happens."

She laughed, untangled herself from his hold and got
up. She stood above him. "Are you serious? In business
together, me and you?"

"Yeah. Is that so crazy?"

She propped her hands on her bare hips and blew
out a breath. Her eyes cinched at the corners, then
she pointed a manicured finger at him. "This can't
be you—some man—running the show. It has to be
a real partnership, not you thinking that you're coming to my rescue. 'Cause I do pretty well on my own,
ya know." She stomped over to the table by the window and picked up a magazine and brought it back to
the bed. She dropped down next to him. "I'm on the
Forty Under Forty list of up-and-coming businesses,
my love." She flipped open to the page with the list and
pointed to her name.

Montgomery let go of the smile he'd been holding in
while she'd read him her version of the riot act. "I would
never doubt it, baby. You're incredible." He leaned in
and kissed her. "You deserve it."

"I've done well here in France. I've built a solid reputation and requests to take on more work. I could have
come home and just fixed everything like I've always
done. Take out a loan to cover the debt, another mort-
gage to save the house, but when I found out about your
project, I saw that as the way out. I knew if I got the
job with my skill and on merit I could save the family
business by bringing *in* the business to make it solvent
again, not just come in on the white horse and save
the day with black girl magic." She looked him right

in the eyes. "And I needed to prove to my father that I had what it takes and had it all along." She dragged in a breath. "I gave you that thank-you card because I wanted you to know that it was never my intent to use you. I went about it all ass-backward but…"

"I don't even know what to say about you, woman," he murmured in awe.

She laughed. "If your offer to partner is still open…"

"Is that something you really want to do? Seems like you're doing pretty well on your own," he quipped, teasing.

She curled next to him. "I think we would make an unstoppable team. We could take our game international."

He slowly nodded, processing the idea. "I like it."

"My brilliance and your good looks…"

He grabbed her up and rolled her on top of him. "Gotta use what you got," he said and pushed inside her to seal the deal.

That evening Lexington took Montgomery on a tour of her little town of Saint-Germain-en-Laye, regaling him with its rich history. They wandered in and out of quaint shops, sat at an outdoor cafe and sipped wine and talked and shared and walked and talked some more. She took him to the Musée du Quai Branly where she'd been commissioned for the restoration work and promised to let him see her handiwork the following day, which they did. And he was once again astounded by her skill. He met her Paris assistants, Danielle Bovant and Celeste Castle, who were clearly the French counterparts to the DC team.

In the three days that they spent together they became the poster couple for the *Paris Is for Lovers* mantra. But all too soon it was time for him to return to the States.

"I'll be there for the opening," she said at the departure gate at Charles de Gaulle Airport. "Ashanti said they're putting on the finishing touches."

"Promise me," he said, cupping her cheeks in his palms.

"I promise. I wouldn't miss it. I want to see my vision come to life."

"I'm going to *miss you* like crazy." He lowered his head and tenderly kissed her. "I love you."

"I love you," she whispered back.

"I'll call you when we land."

All she could do was nod, not trusting her voice. She waved and blew kisses until he was swallowed up by departing passengers.

Six Weeks Later

The days leading up to the grand opening of Essex House were a beehive of activity and contagious energy, combined with the gaiety of the Christmas holiday season. An enormous Christmas tree sat majestically in the center of the lobby. Every inch of the building was photographed, chairs adjusted, pictures hung, flowers arranged and pillows fluffed by Lexington's design team, Ashanti and Nia. And everything from floorboards to light fixtures, doorknobs, and faucets to window frames was inspected by Montgomery's construction management crew now overseen by Hank Forbes—recently promoted to project manager after Montgomery unceremoniously fired Gabriel upon his return from Paris.

"I wish you could have seen his face," he'd told Lexington over the phone. "When I told him I knew it was him that had intentionally leaked the information about your company finances to get back at you, he actually had the nerve to say, 'It was probably one of those ex-cons you hired.' I should have knocked the smug look off his face."

Lexington had scoffed. Typical Gabe. Like he tried to blame Michelle for their affair like he was some hapless dupe. "Always ready to shift the blame," she'd said.

He was very satisfied that he'd given the spot to Hank and he planned to talk with him about his future with MG Holdings.

"Just a couple of hours until showtime," Sterling said, sidling up next to his cousin at the Essex House bar.

"Yep. We did it, man. We really did it."

Sterling clapped him on the back. "Congratulations. This place is going to change lives."

Montgomery exhaled a long breath, nodded and smiled. "That's the plan."

"What time is Lexi getting here?"

"She's coming straight from the airport. Her plane landed a half hour ago. I sent a car for her. She should be here soon," he added, his gaze darting toward the entrance.

"Look at you," he teased, hugging him with his elbow. "All in love." He chuckled.

Montgomery ducked his head. "Feels good. Ya know. Didn't think it could happen for me again."

"When we least expect it, my brother. Take it from one who found out the loooong way. All work and no play made for a not so fulfilling life."

"For real. You wanting to settle has the whole family buzzing. If I hadn't seen you two together with my own eyes I wouldn't believe it myself."

"Ashanti has changed my whole mind."

"The whooole mind?" he teased, making size gestures with his hands.

"Yeah. The whole damned thing."

They slapped palms and shared a long laugh.

"Hey, fellas." Alonzo, Montgomery's brother, joined them.

"Everything good?"

"Good? What…you got *the* man supervising in your—I must say crazy fab—kitchen. No worries. Your guests are gonna be blown away by my menu. Still a little jet-lagged but it's all good."

Alonzo had flown in a day earlier from Abu Dhabi where he'd cooked for the wedding of a dignitary's daughter. But he'd had his contacts in DC begin all the prep work days before.

"I really have to thank Mikayla for pitching in," Montgomery said.

Alonzo's wife, Mikayla, had offered the services of her housekeeping staff to ensure that every apartment and all the common rooms were cleaned and in sparkling shape. Her once upon a time one-woman business, At Your Service, had mushroomed to a staff of two hundred, with locations on the East and West Coasts.

"She was happy to do it. We're family." He draped his arm around his brother's shoulder. "Big brother

Franklin is on his way. He said Dina is moving a little slow these days. The baby is due in like a month."

"Humph. Two kids in three years. When do they have time to do their doctor thing, saving lives and whatnot?" Montgomery joked.

The trio shared a laugh.

It was great that his family was there and that within a couple of hours the rooms would overflow with guests, the new residents, the media, his entire crew and staff. But the only person he cared about seeing was Lexington.

And there she was. She'd paused for a moment when she'd come through the glass-and-chrome doors to take in the space. Her gaze rose upward—her vision of the circular interior had come to life. He watched as her eyes lit up and a slow smile of satisfaction curved that luscious mouth. She turned her head and saw him, and literally dropped her bag in the middle of the lobby and ran across the black-and-white marble floor into his arms.

He didn't care who was looking or that Stella's camera crew was filming everything within range. He wrapped the love of his life in his arms and kissed her and held her and murmured how much he loved and missed her. And she gave back as good as she got.

"Hey, y'all need to get a room," Alonzo yelled.

Laughing, they eased apart. Montgomery held her to his side. "Babe, this is my brother Alonzo. Zo, this is Lexington Randall."

She held out her hand. "Oh, the celebrity chef in the flesh," she teased. "I heard great things about you. You have an amazing life."

Alonzo shook her hand, his gaze shifting between his brother and Lexington. "Yep, yep. I like her, bruh. She's a keeper."

Monty playfully pushed him aside.

"So, what am I, yesterday's lunch?" Sterling playfully grumbled with his arms open for a hug.

Lexington stepped into his hug. "How are you, Sterling? You keeping this one out of trouble?"

"Scout's honor."

"Want to take a look around?" Montgomery whispered in her ear. "I blocked off one of the rooms."

Her eyes twinkled. "How much time do we have?"

He took her hand, instructed the bellhop to get her bag and they headed toward the elevators.

The hostesses and concierges and two live bands were in position in the lobby. Out in front of Essex House, a humming crowd had gathered that stretched along the whole block. The chill of the air warmed by the crush of bodies. Television cameras and print media flanked the swelling throng as everyone waited for the official ribbon cutting.

Lexington gripped Montgomery's hand, her eyes filled with love and pride in all that had been accomplished. She fully acknowledged her part in the almost destruction of their relationship, but she vowed that there would never be a day that she would keep anything from him again.

The couple were embraced on either side of them by their staff and team members that helped bring the day to fruition.

One of Stella's crew members adjusted a standing microphone in front of Montgomery. She gave Montgomery a sincere smile and a thumbs-up as he stepped to the mic.

"Good afternoon, everyone. Thank you all for being here. This is a great day for DC, for our black community."

A roar of applause filled the late afternoon air.

"When my cousin Sterling and I," he gave Sterling a nod of recognition, "starting thinking about how we could make a positive impact on the community we knew that we needed to leverage what came natural to us, real estate development. One of our biggest concerns was the lack of truly affordable housing in the DC area. We also knew that we didn't simply want to throw up a pretty building—we wanted to create a community that the residents and everyone in the surrounding area would be proud of and willing to work to maintain."

More applause.

"So, we put together an incredible team from construction workers, to vendors to the amazing design team." He reached for Lexington's hand and brought her next to him. "And it is the vision of Lexington Randall and her amazing assistants that took ideas on paper and transformed this once neighborhood eyesore into the jewel of DC."

More applause and cheers.

"Essex House has residential as well as rental units, a full gym, onsite parking, underground shopping, a full restaurant and bar, concierge services. The adjacent building is scheduled to open next spring as a community center that will offer after-school programs, tutoring, voter registration and health service referrals."

Lexington squeezed his hand.

"And because we all firmly believe in promoting, supporting and encouraging the black community, all of our workers, staff, vendors are black and/or people of color. And we will continue to support our own, and build communities that thrive and can sustain themselves. Finally, with the vision of self-determination and community building, I have partnered with Lexington Randall of Randall Architect and Design to form L&M Enterprises. This partnership will allow us to consolidate our resources, expertise and vision to continue to create affordable homes, businesses and community spaces for us, by us!"

The clapping and shouting this time was so long and sustained that Montgomery finally had to hold up his hand and beg the enthusiastic group to join him in cutting the ribbon.

He handed Lexington a pair of giant faux gold scissors and a pair to Sterling.

"One. Two. Three."

In unison they cut the ribbon.

"Welcome to Essex House," he shouted, just as soft crystals of snow began to fall.

The guests flowed in, met when they entered by the soft sounds of the live band and greeted by a waiter or waitress with a plate of hors d'oeuvres. Other staff hired for the night, with an Essex House emblem on their black shirts, handed out pamphlets detailing the amenities and giving directions. Social media guru Cara

Mack kept her eye and finger on the pulse of the media and organized the string of interviews for Montgomery and Lexington and was thrilled to see that the opening had gone viral on Twitter. She even convinced Montgomery to say a few words on Instagram live, insisting that a generation of influencers needed to know what he was doing and that change was possible.

For the evening there was an open bar and waiter service at the food stations that ran along the perimeter of the restaurant. Alonzo had outdone himself which he had no problem teasing his brother about.

Today was a day of celebration, the culmination of months and months of hard work, sacrifice and determination. It was not a night to nurse old grudges, and ill feelings so the invitation that Lexington had extended to her father and her brother came from her heart. And even though she still gave her brother the side-eye, he'd promised to make good by being a success at where his passion was, the same way that she did, and would start making restitution to her. Her dad seemed to have made best friends with Montgomery's parents as they were seen laughing it up and sharing a table in the dining room. Since they'd arrived at the decision to bury all the old hatchets, Monty had extended an invitation to Gabriel, who declined, which probably was just as well.

Lexington eased up behind Montgomery and slid her arm around his waist, just as he was finishing up talking with Melissa and Greg Williams. He introduced the long-married couple to Lexington.

"So nice to meet you."

"They've been married over thirty years," Montgomery said with a lift of his brow.

"Wow. How do you make it work?"

"She's always right," Greg said, then hugged his wife when she poked him in the side.

"The truth is," Melissa said, "besides me being right, is that you need to have something that bonds you together, more than being in love, but a passion for something in common."

Lexington nodded as she listened. "Tell me..." she said, wide-eyed. "What's the passion that you two share?"

"Running our B and B. We found we loved taking care of other people and providing a comfortable place for them to stay," Melissa said.

"I'd love to visit sometime."

The couple looked at each other curiously.

"Uh, it was going to be a surprise, Lexi. I thought it would be great for us to get away for the night and just unwind and be catered to."

"Sounds perfect," she said, staring into his eyes. "I can't wait," she mouthed.

"We'll see you two later," Greg said. "We're going to head back."

"Thank you for inviting us. And congratulations," Melissa said. She squeezed his arm and looked at Lexington. "You have someone really special here."

Lexington slid her gaze toward Montgomery. "I know," she said softly.

It was nearly eight by the time Montgomery and Lexington were able to sneak out, leaving the wind down of the grand opening in the capable hands of Sterling and the crew.

Montgomery had a driver waiting out front, his overnight bag and her suitcase had already been loaded into the trunk. The snow had stopped leaving a light coating on the streets.

"You really did have this all planned," Lexington said as she curled next to him in the wide back seat.

He stroked her hair and kissed the top of her head. "You deserve it." He kissed the top of her head again.

The chauffeured car cruised along the winding driveway that opened onto a home that looked to belong in a magazine.

Montgomery got out and helped Lexington to her feet.

"This is gorgeous," she said. "Late eighteen hundreds," she murmured, her architect eye snapping images in her mind.

He took her hand just as Greg and Melissa came out onto the sprawling porch waving at their arrival.

"Welcome, welcome," Melissa greeted. "We are so glad to have you."

"Thank you," Lexington said.

"Come on in and get settled," Greg said. He led the group inside.

The driver brought the bags in. "Call whenever you're ready, Mr. Grant."

"Thanks, Mike."

The couple followed Melissa and Greg and were thrilled to be offered a flute of champagne.

"To the happy couple," Melissa said.

"To continued success," Greg added.

They all raised and touched glasses.

"Let me show you to your room," Melissa offered. "I'm sure you want to unwind after the day you've had," she said to Lexington. "I hear you came from Paris just today."

"Yes, I'd love to get out of these heels and change," she said smiling.

"Right this way." She linked her arm through Lexington's. "Let's leave the men. I'll give you a quick tour on the way to your room."

They stopped in two of the unoccupied rooms. Each one was decorated around a theme. One was the literary suite, complete with original editions of black writers and the walls boasting portraits of Baldwin, Morrison and Walker. The other was dedicated to the ancestors. Bold orange and yellow coverings and pillows, African art and hand-carved statues adorned the spacious room.

"How long have you had this place? It's simply stunning."

"We've managed the property for almost five years, but just recently we became owners," she said proudly.

"Really? Congratulations."

"Would have never happened without Monty."

"What do you mean?" she asked as she stroked the gleaming mahogany bannister.

"He didn't tell you?"

"Tell me? No."

She scoffed. "He is too modest. Changed our lives and the lives of our grandchildren." She went on to explain how Montgomery had deeded them the house and all its contents, fully paid, with the hope that they would now have property that they could pass along to their grandchildren, creating generational wealth.

Lexington would have cried if she didn't want to make a fool of herself in front of a woman she barely knew. *Monty.* Knowing this only made her love him all the more.

"Here we are," Melissa said, opening the door. "This is our suite for lovers." She giggled.

Lexington felt her cheeks heat.

An enormous four-poster bed dominated the room, set on a white fur rug. Romance novels lined a bookshelf, and the soft-white walls held photography of Gordon Parks and the art of Basquiat. Scented lavender candles soothed the air. And floor-to-ceiling windows opened to the terrace.

Melissa opened another door to the master bath complete with a dressing area, Jacuzzi tub and rain-head shower.

"This is…beautiful."

"I'm glad you like it. The phone on the nightstand rings downstairs. Anything you need, just let me know."

"Thank you so much."

Melissa suddenly stepped to her and hugged her. "You'll have the thirty years, too," she said softly.

She stepped back and Lexington blinked away the sting of tears. It was like being hugged by her mother so very long ago. She sniffed. "I hope so," she said.

"I'll let you get settled." She whisked away, closing the door softly behind her.

Slowly Lexington stripped out of her clothes, walked into the bathroom and ran the tub to get ready for her man.

* * *

They shared a steamy scented bath together, and wrapped in thick terry cloth robes they sat in front of the glass terrace doors and watched the moon just beyond the treetops. They sipped on glasses of wine, and held hands, talking quietly about the amazing day and the possibilities for the future.

Montgomery put down his glass and angled his body toward Lexington.

"I've been thinking," he began slowly, hesitantly, "that we should be more than business partners, and since Randall Architect and Design's last *official* job was the Essex House…"

Lexington held her breath.

Montgomery got up and knelt in front of her, looked into her eyes. "I love you, from the bottom of my soul. Every day with you makes me want to see the next and the next with you at my side." He swallowed and reached into the pocket of his robe. He took out a black box and opened it. The diamond set on a platinum band gleamed in the moonlight. "Marry me."

Lexington's eyes widened. Her throat tightened. She leaned forward and slid out of her chair and was on her knees in front of him. She cupped his face in her hands. "I've waited for this kind of love all my life. Someone who loves me for me. I want to spend the next thirty years and then some with you."

He released the breath he'd held and slid the ring on her finger.

She tossed her head back and laughed with pure joy, then wrapped her arms around his neck and sealed their future with a kiss.

And as she held her life-partner-to-be, she thought about what bloomed between them, what they'd created six weeks earlier in Paris. She'd save that bit of joy for the morning. Right now, all she wanted was to make all-night love to her man, as the snow began to fall again, christening their forever.

* * * * *

#2839 WHAT HE WANTS FOR CHRISTMAS
Westmoreland Legacy: The Outlaws • by Brenda Jackson
After a decade apart, COO Sloan Outlaw isn't looking to get back with ex Lesley Cassidy. But with her company facing a hostile takeover, he offers his assistance...if she joins him at his luxury cabin. But when they find themselves snowed in, the heat ignites...

#2840 HOW TO HANDLE A HEARTBREAKER
Texas Cattleman's Club: Fathers and Sons • by Joss Wood
Gaining independence from her wealthy family, officer and law student Hayley Lopez is rarely intimidated, especially by the likes of billionaire playboy developer Jackson Michaels. An advocate for the underdog, Hayley clashes often with Jackson. But will one hot night together change everything?

#2841 THE WRONG MR. RIGHT
Dynasties: The Carey Center • by Maureen Child
For contractor Hannah Yates, the offer to work on CEO Bennett Carey's project is a boon. Hired to repair his luxury namesake restaurant, she finds his constant presence and good looks...distracting. Burned before, she won't lose focus, but the sparks between them can't be ignored...

#2842 HOLIDAY PLAYBOOK
Locketts of Tuxedo Park • by Yahrah St. John
Advertising exec Giana Lockett has a lot to prove to her football dynasty family, and landing sports drink CEO Wynn Starks's account is crucial. But their undeniable attraction is an unforeseen complication. Will they be able to make the winning play to save their relationship and business deal?

#2843 INCONVENIENT ATTRACTION
The Eddington Heirs • by Zuri Day
When wealthy businessman Cayden Barker is blindsided by Avery Gray, it's not just by her beauty—her car accidently hits his. And then they meet again unexpectedly—at the country club where he's a member and she's employed. Is this off-limits match meant to last?

#2844 BACKSTAGE BENEFITS
Devereaux Inc. • by LaQuette
TV producer Josiah Manning needs to secure lifestyle guru Lyric Smith as host of his new show. As tempting as the offer—and producer—is, Lyric is hesitant. But as a rival emerges, will they take the stage together or let the curtain fall on their sizzling chemistry?

---

*After a decade apart, COO Sloan Outlaw
isn't looking to get back with ex Lesley Cassidy.
But with her company facing a hostile takeover,
he offers his assistance...if she joins him at his luxury
cabin. But when they find themselves snowed in,
the heat ignites...*

Read on for a sneak peek at
What He Wants for Christmas
by New York Times *bestselling author Brenda Jackson.*

"What do you want to ask me, Sloan?"

He drew in a deep breath. "I need to know what made you come looking for me last night."

She broke eye contact with him and glanced out the window, not saying anything for a moment. "You were gone longer than you said you would be. I got worried. It was either go see what was taking you so long or pace the floor with worry even more. I chose the former."

"But the weather had turned into a blizzard, Les." He then realized he'd called her what he'd normally called her while they'd been together. She had been Les and not Leslie.

"I know that. I also knew you were out there in it. I tried to convince myself that you could take care of yourself, but I also knew with the amount of wind blowing and snow coming down that anything could have happened."

She paused again before saying, "Chances are, you would have made it back to the cabin, but I couldn't risk the chance you would not have."

He tried not to concentrate on the sadness he heard in her voice and saw in her eyes. Instead, he concentrated on her mouth and in doing so was reminded of just how it tasted. "Not sure if I would have made it back, Les. My head was hurting, and it was getting harder and harder to make my body move because I was so cold. Hell, I wasn't even sure I was going in the right direction. I regret you put your own life at risk, but I'm damn glad you were there when I needed you."

"Just like you were there for me and my company when I needed you, Sloan," she said softly.

Her words made him realize that they'd been there for each other when it had mattered the most. He didn't want to think what would have been the outcome if he'd been at the cabin alone as originally planned and the snowstorm hit. Nor did he want to think what would have happened to her and her company if Redford hadn't told him what was going on. The potential outcome of either made him shiver.

"You're still cold. I'd better go and get that hot chocolate going," she said, shifting to get up and reach for her clothes.

"Don't go yet," he said, not ready for any distance to be put between them or their bodies.

She glanced over at him. Their gazes held and then, as if she'd just noticed his erection pressing against her thigh, she said, "You do know the only reason why we're naked in this sleeping bag together, right?"

He nodded. "Yes. Because I needed your body's heat last night." He inched his mouth closer to hers and then said, "Only problem is, I still need your body's heat, Les. But now I need it for a totally different reason."

And then he leaned in and kissed her.

Don't miss what happens next in…
What He Wants for Christmas *by Brenda Jackson,*
the next book in her Westmoreland Legacy:
The Outlaws series!

Available December 2021 wherever
Harlequin Desire books and ebooks are sold.

Harlequin.com

IF YOU ENJOYED THIS BOOK
WE THINK YOU WILL ALSO LOVE

⬧ HARLEQUIN

PRESENTS

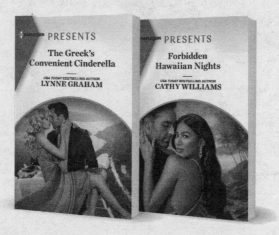

Escape to exotic locations where passion knows no bounds.

Welcome to the glamorous lives of royals and billionaires, where passion knows no bounds. Be swept into a world of luxury, wealth and exotic locations.

8 NEW BOOKS AVAILABLE EVERY MONTH!

Love Harlequin romance?

DISCOVER.

Be the first to find out about promotions, news and exclusive content!

 Facebook.com/HarlequinBooks

 Twitter.com/HarlequinBooks

 Instagram.com/HarlequinBooks

 Pinterest.com/HarlequinBooks

You Tube YouTube.com/HarlequinBooks

ReaderService.com

EXPLORE.

Sign up for the Harlequin e-newsletter and download a free book from any series at **TryHarlequin.com**

CONNECT.

Join our Harlequin community to share your thoughts and connect with other romance readers!
Facebook.com/groups/HarlequinConnection

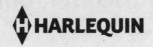

HARLEQUIN

Heartfelt or thrilling, passionate or uplifting—Harlequin is more than just happily-ever-after.

With twelve different series to choose from and new books available every month, you are sure to find stories that will move you, uplift you, inspire and delight you.

HNEWS2021